Coyote Stories

By Mourning Dove (Humishuma)

Edited and illustrated by Heister Dean Guie
with notes by L. V. McWhorter (Old Wolf)
and a foreword by Chief Standing Bear

Introduction and notes to the Bison Book Edition
by Jay Miller

University of Nebraska Press
Lincoln and London

First Bison Book printing: 1990

Library of Congress Cataloging-in-Publication Data
Mourning Dove. 1888–1936.
Coyote stories / by Mourning Dove (Humishuma): edited and illustrated
by Heister Dean Guie, with notes by L. V. McWhorter (Old Wolf) and a
foreword by Chief Standing Bear.
p.   cm.
Reprint. Originally published: Caldwell, Idaho: Caxton Printers, 1933.
ISBN 0-8032-3145-8.   ISBN 0-8032-8169-2 (pbk.)
1. Coyote (Legendary character) 2. Okinagan Indians—Legends. 3.
Tales—Washington (State) I. Guie, Heister Dean. II. Title.
E99.O35M68   1990
398.24′52974442—dc20
89-28956 CIP

Originally published by The Caxton Printers, Ltd., Caldwell, Idaho, in
1933. Restored to this Bison Book edition are three stories that did not appear in the first edition. They were reconstructed from memory by the author's half-brother.

♾

INTRODUCTION TO THE BISON BOOK EDITION
By Jay Miller

Coyote Stories consumed the final years of Christine Quintasket, who wrote under the name of Mourning Dove (sometimes she used *Humishuma*, the Colville-Okanogan term for "mourning dove").[1] She was an enrolled member of the Colville Reservation of north-central Washington. With little schooling and less exposure to literature, she early determined to become a writer of fiction, particularly western novels. Prior to her efforts, Indian women authors like Pauline Johnson and Zitkala-Ša (Gertrude Simmons Bonin) had devoted themselves to short stories. Earning money as a migrant laborer or housekeeper, Mourning Dove wrote every day. Even on days when she spent ten hours packing apples, she wrote into the night, long after other exhausted workers had gone to sleep.

After drafting her only full novel about 1912, she put it away until, several years later, she met Lucullus Virgil McWhorter, a Yakima Valley businessman sympathetic to Indian causes, and they began to collaborate on a final version.[2] Finished in 1916, *Cogewea* was not published until 1927. During the interim, Mourning Dove was encouraged to record the stories and traditions of her people, the Interior Salish.[3]

Though initially reluctant, Mourning Dove soon warmed to the task of collecting "folklores," as she always called her subject. She had heard stories her entire life from relatives and visiting elders. Once motivated, she deliberately sought out aged members of other communities to hear, and afterward record, their stories. Most nights, she either carefully wrote stories she had heard that evening or reworked legends collected previously. When satisfied, she sent or took bundles of them to Yakima for McWhorter to edit.

To help her with spelling, agreement, and grammar, McWhorter introduced her to Heister Dean Guie, who wrote for the Yakima city newspaper. Beginning as silent editor, Guie became increasingly involved in the project. He and Mourning Dove passed letters to each other through McWhorter, who sometimes had to smooth out difficulties. Guie was after consistency and returned, again and again, to the same points, much to the frustration of Mourning Dove. He asked for the identifications and spellings of animal names in Salishan languages, for the pattern number (Was it three or five?), and for details of dress and ornament. Eventually, he did drawings to illustrate characters, depicting their animal characterizations over their spirit and human aspects. Guie also convinced the others that these stories should be written "for the children of another race to read" (as Mourning Dove said at the end of the Preface).

As she did in the stories, Mourning Dove fashioned an expurgated version of her life for the public. A version of it appears in her Preface, where she dates her birth to 1888 and says her father's father was "a Hudson's Bay Company man, a hardy, adventurous Celt." The reservation censuses and her father's other children, however, deny these claims.

Christine Quintasket was first named on the tribal census of 30 June 1891, where she was listed as eight years old, and she was shown to be the same age on the roll for 1893. Since she was always large for her age, I judge that she was born about 1885. A decade later, she was enrolled briefly as Christine Joseph by her parents in the Sacred Heart/Colville/Goodwin Mission School at Ward, Washington, near Kettle Falls. She quickly became ill and was taken home by her father. A major portion of her trauma was the result of the school's insistence that she speak only English. Previously she had spoken only Salish, but now she was punished for doing so by the nuns, who, incongruously, were themselves native speakers of French. She enrolled again, successfully, from about 1896 to 1899, when she made her First Communion. In 1900 all native students were transferred to the government school at Fort Spokane. In 1902 her mother, Lucy Stuikin, died and Christine went home to care for her siblings. After her father, Joseph Quintasket, married Cecilia Williams in 1904, Christine found employment for three years at Fort Shaw Indian School near Great Falls, Montana, where she could attend classes and visit her grandmother, Maria, who was living among the Kootenay at Tobacco Plains. In 1908 she witnessed the roundup of the last wild bison herd in the United States, and, from hints in her writings, seems to have had a religious vision involving a buffalo skull.

At Fort Shaw she met Hector McLeod, married him in 1909, and went to live at Polson. The marriage was rocky, and Christine often lived away from him. In 1912 she moved to Portland, where she apparently assumed the pen name of Morning Dove, a character in Salishan legends associated with the dawn (new beginnings) and faithfulness, and drafted her novel, partially in reaction to the treatment of Indians in contemporary Western writings.[4]

To gain greater facility with written English, she attended a Calgary business college in 1913–15. The next year, she was the school teacher on the Inkameep Reserve in British Columbia. Her younger sister had married into the chiefly family there and the sisters enjoyed living among their father's Okanagan relatives, just north of the Colville Reservation. While she was teaching, Christine's nights were devoted to revising and finishing her novel, *Cogewea*, with the help of McWhorter, who also urged her to begin collecting native stories. She did so, although both she and McWhorter erred in thinking that Salishan legendary history was quickly disappearing.

On 8 September 1919, she married Fred Galler, a Wenatchi, and settled at East Omak on the western edge of the Colville Reservation, when they were not camping in orchards and fields as migrant laborers. Once back on the reservation, she became increasingly involved in native rights, bridging the differences between her people and their white neighbors.

Although many locals were suspicious of her literary efforts, her name was often in the press as a regional celebrity. During a museum visit in December 1921, she learned that the correct ornithological spelling for her pen name was Mourning Dove. She adopted that spelling, with all of its tragic overtones.

She continued to move around the Inland Empire, taking on odd jobs with her husband, collecting folklores, and writing. Her novel was slow to appear, and she was often vexed with the publisher. Still, she persisted. When it did come out in 1927, she became a more public figure, although known only by her pen or married names, despite the fact that most Colvilles knew her as Quintasket.

She joined with other native women to found social and handiwork clubs, and began to speak out about native rights and agency abuses. She also joined with other Colvilles to have the oversized agency staff reduced. An agency farming instructor whose job was threatened attacked Christine's literary aspirations by spreading word that she had not written her novel but had only allowed her pen name to be used as a front for its white author, presumably McWhorter. Greatly angered, Christine received an apology from this agency farmer, just before he lost his job. Years later, they became neighbors and friends.

Driven more than ever, with fatal consequences for her health, she set out to prove her own abilities and drafted versions of her autobiography. It has now been edited and published[5] after half a century in storage.

She joined with other activists in 1930 to found the Colville Indian Association, seeking payments still outstanding from unresolved land claims. They also became concerned with the alleged misuse of tribal monies. In 1933 she reminded a company leasing land on the reservation that it had not met its commitment to hire tribal members. In May 1935 she became the first woman elected to the Colville Tribal Council.

Her political efforts and her persistent writing took their toll. Christine Galler was taken to a state asylum on 30 July and died there on 8 August 1936 at 10:15 p.m. Much of the time she was delirious, reliving fearsome encounters with the Devil she had first experienced during a bout with influenza in 1918. The cause of death was listed as "exhaustion from manic psychosis," and her occupation was given as housewife and authoress. Her father, Joseph, outlived her. Throughout her life, she had been careful to shield him from her literary audience. Largely, this was to protect his privacy, but, in part, it was also to avoid questions about her claim that Joseph's father had been Irish or Scots. He was always listed as a full blood on the tribal rolls. Both his parents were Okanagans, although his mother also had ties with the Nicola, a tiny Athapaskan-speaking group since assimilated among Salishans. Given the tenor of the times and region, her claims to some white ancestry probably gave her more freedom to move among her neighbors and to appeal to a broader readership.

Thus, despite claims of traditional authenticity, Mourning Dove's legends are not true to Salishan recitations. They have been sanitized, and the portions that she called "ugly" have been removed. Nor are they as casual or spontaneous as they would be in native settings. Fearful for the demise of these stories, Salishans today continue to tell them, albeit in English rather than native languages. Elders will sometimes remind each other of stories and compare notes on distinctive family versions. The best Coyote stories are usually heard at wakes, while family and friends are sitting up all night with the deceased. During the darkest of the night, old ladies will begin to tell the most outrageous stories, helping to relieve the grief and keep everyone awake.

Stories can only be told when they do not interfere with more vital activities. Thus, they are usually limited to winter evenings. Exceptions are permitted, however, among leading families when they are passing a site mentioned in legend. Then it is very appropriate to relate the story while surrounded by landmarks mentioned in it.

The audience is as fully involved with the recitation as the speaker; they all have roles to play. During public narratives, listeners must periodically respond to indicate they are paying attention and to encourage the storyteller. For the Interior Salish, the usual response was the sound used for the affirmative, which was also the predominant vowel of these dialect chains. Moving up the Columbia River from Vantage, the "ay" chain consisted of the Columbians, Wenatchis (Peskwaws), Entiats, and Chelans; the Methows used a distinctive "ii" but historically were adopting the "ay"; and the Okanogans, Nespelems, Sanpoils, Colviles (Kettle Falls), and Arrow Lakes used the "aa". These tribes, mostly occupying tributaries of the Columbia River from prehistoric times, eventually settled on the Colville Reservation. To the east, the Spokans, Kalispels, and Flatheads (the original Salish) used an "ae" diphthong like that in "bat". Although these features of Salish oral literature are important for understanding the performance aspects of this tradition, they were not considered necessary for the literary presentation intended by Mourning Dove and her editors.

Though concerned with the decorum of these stories, Mourning Dove did include some carry-overs and hints from the traditional contexts, but she carefully avoided calling attention to them. Her treatment of Coyote is particularly cursory, requiring further explication.

Coyote is a complex figure, often baffling to a white audience. He is more anti-hero than hero, more buffoon than champion. He is, for native people, the ultimate negative example, sharing this distinction with other trickster-transformer figures such as Hare in the East, Raven in the Northwest, and Spider in the Plains. Like them, he is Everyone, a native version of the medieval European Everyman, expanded beyond the human species to encompass all of sapient life. His greatest flaw is pride and self-importance. Among the Interior Salish, he is known by two names, although Mourning Dove uses only *Sin-ka-lip*, the most common term. When the stories are told in a Salishan language, however, Coyote refers to himself as Smyaw, derived from a root meaning "important."[6]

Throughout the Americas, not just among the Salishans, the original inhabitants of the world were indeed people, but they were other-than-human and amorphous. Their essential form was that which later became restricted to the human species, with arms, legs, hands, head, and overall vulnerability. In addition, these primal people also had the attributes of spirits and of species. Sometimes, they are described as shimmering and iridescent. Through tricks of light and shadow, they could change shape and attributes as need or whim arose.

Things remained inchoate during the time of most of the legends. Somehow, these people began to sense that a change was coming because, as so many stories say, "Humans are coming soon." To plan for the arrival of the "new people," a council was held, convened by the leader of that world. It is this council that is the subject of the first story in Mourning Dove's book, albeit in abbreviated version.

For Colville elders of today the fullest account says that all of the people met to decide the names and activities each would assume in the new age. For example, Salmon and Bear agreed to offer their flesh to humans in return for careful treatment and respect. Other people went off in a huff and threatened dire consequences for humans, becoming known as people eaters. It was these renegades and monsters who had to be tamed before humans could settle down.

In the most sacred version, the leader had a pole stacked with rings in front of him. Each ring represented a name and a lifeway. At the very bottom of the pole was the ring intended for Coyote, a ne'er-do-well if there ever was one. As described, Coyote intended to stay up all night and be the first one at the dawn council so as to assume a more exalted position than his actions had hitherto merited. Instead, he fell asleep and his wife, the ever faithful Mole, did not disturb him. After waking, he rushed to the meeting place demanding a great name. The leader was so impressed by Coyote's ability to think for himself, although to selfish ends, that he reversed the pole and put Coyote in charge of finishing up the world.

In some version, when all was set, the leader himself, not his wife as Mourning Dove said, decreed that he would help humans in the future by becoming Sweatlodge, the place for purification, prayer, and petition. He had no head, arms, or legs as Sweatlodge and so Coyote became his substitute.

As he bestowed every one of the names, the leader also gave out medicine powers. He would point to the center of a person's body, to the heart, which is the seat of thought and emotions,[7] and proclaim what that power would be. Typically, Coyote misunderstood this gesture, assuming that the leader was pointing at his stomach. Thus, by virtue of the creative force granted to his thoughts, Coyote received a special power different from other beings. The representatives of his power lived in Coyote's intestines until he summoned their help. At that moment, they came out and took the form of five feces or, as polite Colvilles say, turds. Coyote called them his younger siblings and asked their advice, which they always gave wisely, although each encounter always ended with Coyote, suddenly brilliant, claiming that their help was superfluous because, after all, he had known what to do all the time. If his younger siblings were slow or reluctant to offer advice, he bullied them into cooperation by threatening to cause a rainstorm which would melt them.

Here, then, is Coyote at his best and worst: a vastly powerful being who relies on feces to get himself out of difficulties. Moreover, all of his activities are filled with the full range of earthy and physiological processes, especially gluttony, lust, and greed. Throughout, he claims more than he is capable of, regardless of the consequences, often death. As a precaution, Sweatlodge gave Fox, Coyote's kinsman, the ability to restore life by stepping over any shred of bone or fur left of Coyote. Traditionally, Fox had to step over him five times, the ancient pattern number, but with the arrival of Jesuit missionaries and the acceptance of Catholicism, modern accounts mention only three times, the Judeo-Christian pattern number. Throughout these stories, Mourning Dove follows the modern usage of three.

Some of Coyote's escapades are included by Mourning Dove, but a few are not because they might offend white sensibilities. In some cases, she turned episodes within a series of adventures into separate stories; a practice allowed within the creativity of the tradition, however. For any story, the only sure way of knowing that it is over is to have Coyote die at the conclusion. Of course, the next tale begins with Fox restoring Coyote's life so that anything can happen.

Although each Salishan family, band, and tribe had its own version of these stories, there were generalized plots for the most important of the sagas. For Coyote, there are series that describe how he made the world the way it is today, pronouncing the "commandment" at the end of each episode to "set the law" about some present condition.

The most famous of these involved Coyote bringing salmon up the Columbia River and its tributaries.[8] According to most versions, Coyote heard that there were five sisters living near the mouth of the Columbia and keeping wonderful fish in a trap. Coyote wanted to eat these fish, so he went there. Just above the trap, he turned himself into a baby fastened into a cradleboard and floated down the river. The sisters saw him and, having no children of their own, rescued him, although the youngest girl was vocal about her suspicion that the baby was really Coyote. Infused with maternal sentiments, the older sisters paid no attention, alerting the audience to be aware of the youngest-smartest motif so common in Plateau mythology.

Every day the women went out to gather food to eat with their fish and, while they were away, Coyote assumed his usual form and worked on releasing the Salmon. He made five stone bowls and five picks, went down to the trap, and began to dislodge its supports. This went on for some time, with Coyote turning himself back into a baby before the sisters came home each night.

One day, however, the youngest sister could stand it no longer and went back home to test her suspicions. Sure enough, the baby was not there and, looking further, she discovered Coyote dismantling the Salmon trap. Yelling to her sisters that Coyote was stealing their Salmon, she mobilized an attack. Coyote wore a stone bowl like a helmet until it broke under the blows of the sisters; then he put on another. As the last bowl and the last pick broke, the Salmon were released and Coyote led them upriver. Whenever he was hungry, he called a Salmon onto a beach, clubbed it, cooked it, and ate it. By returning the bones to the river, however, the Salmon came back to life and continued upstream.

Coyote, only too typically, soon tired of this easy life and decided to visit the people living in villages at the confluences of tributaries of the Columbia. He entered each village and offered the gift of Salmon in return for a wife while he stayed in the community. The size and number of Salmon sent into local streams were consistent with the beauty of the wife.[9]

Thus, the Colviles at Kettle Falls were most hospitable and received plentiful runs of huge Salmon. The Entiats were less generous, so their river had a brief run of small fish. The Methows were mildly accommodating and gained moderate-sized Salmon. Because the Chelans and Nespelems refused him, their rivers now have waterfalls blocking passage upriver. Furthermore, for every fishery, Coyote also set the techniques and fishing gear to be used. At each locale, what modern elders call the "proof" of such commandments can be found. Often, these are figures drawn on rock faces depicting the use of spears, traps, nets, or weirs. Understandably, the best procedure to use at that place is also the one decreed by Coyote. For example, the size and color specified for a net matched that of water conditions. The use of a spear or leister allowed for limitations of space and sparseness of the run.

At Kettle Falls, where the salmon were huge until Grand

Coulee Dam blocked their return, large basket traps were extremely effective, and the take was shared with anyone who was there at the time of distribution. Failure to share these salmon among one and all violated the local commandment and offended the Salmon people, who would be less likely to return the next year. Hence, complete and total sharing was the rule and practice at the falls.[10]

Nearer Mourning Dove's ancestral home at Piya (Kelly Hill), small salmon went up the Kettle River as far as Cascade Falls. Recently, when biologists tried to introduce landlocked salmon above the falls, they died, and elders remarked that Coyote's commandment forbidding salmon above the falls is still in force.[11]

According to tradition, therefore, each of these stories was localized for all time, a belief known to Mourning Dove only too well, though ignored in print, except in her account of the Hee-Hee Wishing Stone.

Today, various landmarks around the Colville Reservation are explained as the work of Coyote. At Brewster, the domed hill behind the town is known in Salish as Coyote's House, one of many. Steamboat Rock near Grand Coulee Dam is known for the variety of plants growing on its top. These are said to be the result of Coyote stopping there with a basket full of goodies, accidently tipping it over, and angrily commanding that these particular foods stay there. The mesa itself is said by some elders to be the overturned basket. Soap Lake received its greasy consistency when Coyote hid something in its waters and, as one elder put it delicately, "went potty" there so no one could see what was hidden.

Other incidents in the life of Coyote are discussed in the appended commentary on Mourning Dove's versions of each story. While her overall arrangement may seem haphazard, these stories are bracketed between events that were milestones in Coyote's life, Naming Day at its start and the Arrow Trail to the Sky World much later. Afterward, Coyote left the people and moved to the East, some say to a glass-domed house floating in the ocean, from which he will return when he is needed again. Some elders predict a day when Coyote will come back and smash all of the dams built along the Columbia, washing away environmental pollution and once again bringing the Salmon upriver.

As hope for the future and shaper of the past, Coyote's appeal continues unabated among both natives and scholars. One of the most poignant summaries of his attraction comes from the Chemehuevis, a tribe along the Colorado River,[12] who say with chagrin that, while recognizing the many figures of rectitude in their mythology, nevertheless, "We follow Coyote" because "He embodies *all* the human traits: laziness and patient industry or frantic exertion; foolishness and skillful planning; selfishness and concern for others . . . he is the incomplete and the imperfect . . . Coyote has fun, and it is fun to hear about him and his exploits. What he lacks in dignity he makes up in sheer exuberance." Moreover, Coyote is not hopeless. Among the Chinook of the lower Columbia, there was a tendency for Coyote to develop "from a trickster who is impelled by youthful drives, to a conscience-controlled announcer and transformer."[13]

For almost two decades of help, I would like to thank Colville elders Charles Quintasket, Isabel Friedlander Arcasa, TB Charlie, and Juliann Timentwa. Because a sense of place is such a vital component of understanding these works, it seems significant that Coyote and I reached an understanding at Lithia Park in Ashland, Oregon, while Shakespeare hovered in the wings. I would like to dedicate this reissue of Colville stories to the families of Joseph Quintasket, who exemplify Colville traditions at their best.

NOTES

1. Jay Miller, "Mourning Dove: The Author as Cultural Mediator" in *Being and Becoming Indian: Biographical Studies of North American Frontiers* (Chicago: Dorsey Press, 1989), pp. 160–82; *Mourning Dove: A Salishan Au-*

tobiography, ed. Jay Miller (Lincoln: University of Nebraska Press, 1990).

2. Alice Poindexter (Dexter) Fisher, "The Transportation of Tradition: A Study of Zitkala-Ša and Mourning Dove, Two Transitional American Indian Writers," Ph.D. diss., City College of New York, 1979.

3. Nelson Ault, The Papers of Lucullus Virgil McWhorter (Pullman: Friends of the Washington State University, 1959).

4. Compare Theresa Broderick, *The Brand. A Tale of the Flathead Reservation* (Seattle: The Alice Harriman Book Co., 1909).

5. *Mourning Dove: A Salishan Autobiography*, 1990.

6. Compare Anthony Mattina, *Colville-Okanagan Dictionary* (University of Montana Occasional Papers in Linguistics no. 5. 1987), pp. 105, 303.

7. Jay Miller, "The Matter of the (Thoughtful) Heart: Centrality, Focality, or Overlap," *Journal of Anthropological Research*, 36 (Fall 1980): 338–42.

8. Compare Verne Ray, "Native Villages and Groupings of the Columbia Basin," *Pacific Northwest Quarterly*, 27 (1936): 99–152.

9. Compare *Tales of the Okanagans*, ed. Donald M. Hines (Fairfield, Wash.: Ye Galleon Press, 1976).

10. David H. Chance, "Influences of the Hudson's Bay Company on the Native Cultures of the Colville District," *Northwest Anthropological Research Notes, Memoir 2* (1973); Christopher J. Turnbull, "Archaeology and Ethnohistory in the Arrow Lakes, Southeastern British Columbia" (Ottawa: National Museum of Man, Mercury Series 65, 1977); Wayne Suttles, "Plateau Pacifism Reconsidered: Ethnography, Ethnology, and Ethnohistory," in *Coast Salish Essays* (Seattle: University of Washington Press, 1987), pp. 282–86.

11. Compare *Tales of the Okanagans*, p. 25.

12. Carobeth Laird, *The Chemehuevis* (Banning, Calif.: Malki Museum Press, 1976), pp. 231–32.

13. Melville Jacobs, *The Content and Style of an Oral Literature: Clackamas Chinook Myths and Tales*, Viking Fund Publications in Anthropology no. 26 (1959).

Coyote Stories

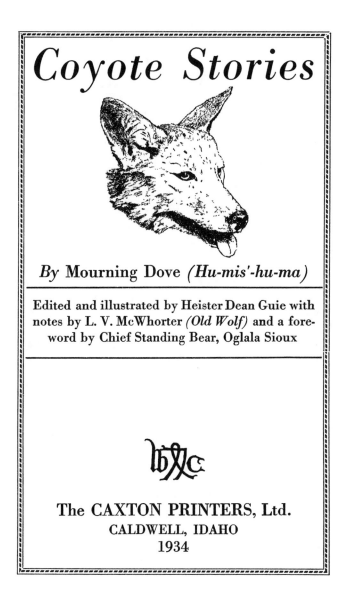

By Mourning Dove *(Hu-mis'-hu-ma)*

Edited and illustrated by Heister Dean Guie with
notes by L. V. McWhorter *(Old Wolf)* and a foreword by Chief Standing Bear, Oglala Sioux

The CAXTON PRINTERS, Ltd.
CALDWELL, IDAHO
1934

MOURNING DOVE (HUMISHUMA)—THE AUTHOR.

FOREWORD

I AM GLAD that Humishuma has written these stories of her people. Since the old Indians in whom these folk-tales are vested are passing away from us, it is good that we bestir ourselves and salvage at least a part of our inheritance. And what a rich store every tribe would have if each had a historian to record its tales!

Story-telling is an ancient profession, and these stories are among our oldest possessions. For many years before the white man ever came to our homeland these legends were told over and over, and handed down from generation to generation. They were our books, our literature, and the memories of the story-tellers were the leaves upon which they were written.

We who lived the days of tribal life before our destruction began remember with gratefulness our story-tellers and the delight and joy and richness which they imparted to our lives. We never tired of their tales, though told countless times. They will, forsooth, never grow old, for they have within them the essence of things that cannot grow old. These legends are of America, as are its mountains, rivers, and forests, and as are its people. They belong!

Story-telling was, and is today, a means of pastime, but the real value of tribal stories lay in the fact that they were closely related to the lives of the people. As history and as literature they became inherited traditions, and they were as wide in their character as the experiences of the people. They told of travels, adventures, and discoveries. In them and through them lived our brave and heroic. There were those that carried lessons and morals for daily guidance. Then, too, there were fairy tales, lovely in their fantasy of thought.

But our legends are passing as the old are passing, and our young are not learning them— which is a part of our destruction. This is sad, especially as the public seems to be becoming somewhat aware of the significance of these tales.

So, in writing the legends of her tribespeople, Humishuma is fulfilling a duty to her fore-fathers, and at the same time she is performing a service to posterity.

These stories are valuable. They will continue to grow more valuable as the years go by, for through the few snatches of recorded song and story the spirit of the Indian will live and breathe, and, though the figure of the American Indian passes forever from the stage of life, the spirit is imperishable.

CHIEF STANDING BEAR.

PREFACE

THE Animal People were here first—before there were any real people.

Coyote was the most important because, after he was put to work by the Spirit Chief, he did more than any of the others to make the world a good place in which to live. There were times, however, when Coyote was not busy for the Spirit Chief. Then he amused himself by getting into mischief and stirring up trouble. Frequently he got into trouble himself, and then everybody had a good laugh—everybody but Mole. She was Coyote's wife.

My people call Coyote *Sin-ka-lip'*, which means Imitator. He delighted in mocking and imitating others, or in trying to, and, as he was a great one to play tricks, sometimes he is spoken of as "Trick Person."

Our name for the Animal People is *Chip-chap-tiqulk* (the "k" barely is sounded), and we use the same word for the stories that are told about the Animal People and legendary times. To the younger generations, *chip-chap-tiqulk* are improbable stories; that is a result of the white man's schools. But to the old Indians, *chip-chap-tiqulk* are not at all improbable; they are accounts of what really happened when the world was very young.

My people are the Okanogan[1] and the *Swhy-ayl'-puh* (Colville), closely related Salishan tribes, and I also have relatives in the *En-koh-tu-me-whoh,* or Nicola, band of the Thompson River Indians in British Columbia. My father's

[1]Okanogan—variously spelled *Okanagon, Okinagan, Oknacken, Oakinacken, Okinakane, etc.*—has the native pronunciation *Okan-nock-kane.* Its translation has puzzled more scholarly heads than mine. Some white writers have said that the word means "rendezvous," applying originally to the head of the Okanogan River at Osoyoos Lake, where the various tribes often gathered. But only the last syllable, *gan* (more properly *kane* or *kain*) has been interpreted. Like our words *kan* and *kin,* it means "head," "tip," or "top."

Now, there is a word, *wickan,* that means "seeing," and *wickanakane* means "seeing-the-head (top or tip)." It is quite possible that *okan* is an ancient variation or contraction of *wickan.* Hence, we could have *Okan-nock-kane* interpreted as "Seeing-the-top." The top of what? Of *Chopaka* (Sticking), a snow peak to the west of the Okanogan Valley. That is what some of the older Indians believe, although they are not positive as to the accuracy of the reference.

Chopaka is visible from a long distance. It is an outstanding topographical feature of the tribe's ancient stamping-grounds.

In the beginning the Okanogan may have designated themselves, or been described by other tribes, as "People-living-where-you-can-see-the-top" (of Chopaka), or as "People-seeing-the-top," the phrase becoming shortened to "Seeing-the-top" *(Wickanakane).*

This explanation I have not seen in print, have never seen it advanced by any of the white people who have investigated. I cannot claim that it is correct, but I consider it as logical and as near the truth, if not nearer, as other guesses that have been submitted.

MOURNING DOVE.

mother was a Nicola, and his father was a Hudson's Bay Company man, a hardy, adventurous Celt. My father, Joseph *Quintasket* (Dark Cloud), was born in the Upper Okanogan community near Kelowna, B. C., but has lived, since a boy, with the Lower Okanogan and the Colville, south of the international boundary. It is with the Lower, or River, Okanogan and the *Swhy-ayl'-puh* on the Colville Reservation in northeastern Washington that I am identified.

The *Swhy-ayl'-puh*—also called *Schu-ayl-pk, Schwelpi* and *Shoyelpee*—became known as the Colville following the establishment of Fort Colville by the Hudson's Bay Company in 1825-26. The fort, named after Andrew Colville, a London governor of the Company, was built near Kettle Falls in the Columbia River, in the heart of the *Swhy-ayl'-puh* country.

My mother's name was Lucy *Stui'-kin*. She was a *Swhy-ayl'-puh* full-blood. Her grandfather was *See-whelh-ken,* who was head chief of the tribe for many years. His nephew, *Kin-kan-nawh,* whom the white people called Pierre Jerome, was chief when the American government made the tribe give up its home in the Colville Valley in 1872 and move to poorer land on the other side of the Columbia. My mother was born at Kettle Falls—the "Big Falls" of these legends—and she and father were married in a log church at that location. The church was built by Indians who had accepted the teachings of the missionaries.

I was born in a canoe on the Kootenai River, near Bonner's Ferry, Idaho, in the Moon of the Leaves (April), 1888. My parents were traveling with a packtrain, which my uncle, Louie *Stui'-kin,* operated between Walla Walla, Washington and Fort Steele, B. C. during the mining rush that year. My mother and grandmother were being ferried across the river when I arrived. The Indian who was paddling their canoe stripped off his shirt and handed it to grandmother, who wrapped me up in it.

It used to be the custom for story-tellers to go from village to village and relate *chip-chaptiqulk* to the children. How gladly were those tribal historians welcomed by busy mothers, and how glad were the boys and girls when one came to visit!

Vividly I recall old *S'whist-kane* (Lost-Head), also known as Old Narciss, and how, in the course of a narrative, he would jump up and mimic his characters, speaking or singing in a strong or weak voice, just as the Animal Persons were supposed to have done. And he would dance around the fire in the tule-mat covered lodge until the pines rang with the gleeful shouts of the smallest listeners. We thought of this as all fun and play, hardly aware that the tale-telling and impersonations were a part of our primitive education.

Another favorite was Broken Nose Abraham. He was old and crippled. He came to our village usually on a white horse, riding double with his blind wife, who held the reins and guided the horse at his direction. It always thrilled us to see Broken Nose ride into camp; he had a stock of such fascinating stories. Broken Nose could not dance for us. He could not even walk without the support of his two canes. But he sang exciting war songs, and we liked to sing with him.

Some of the women were noted story-tellers, but they never made it a business to go from village to village to tell them. We children would go to them. I particularly remember *Ka-at-qhu* (Big Lip), Old Jennie, *Tee-qualt* (Tall), or Long Thresa, and my maternal grandmother, *Soma-how-atqhu* (She-got-her-power-from-the-water). I loved these simple, kindly people, and I think of them often. And in my memory I treasure a picture of my dear mother, who, when I was a very little girl, made the bedtime hours happy for me with the legends she told. She would tell them to me until I fell asleep. Two that are in this collection, "Why Marten's Face Is Wrinkled" and "Why Mosquitoes Bite People," she told over and over again, and I never grew tired of hearing them.

My father always enjoyed telling the old stories, and he does still. He and *Ste-heet-qhu* (Soup), Toma Martin and *Kleen-ment-itqu* are among the few men and women left who can tell *chip-chap-tiqulk*. I thank them for helping me. And I must acknowledge my debt to a blue-eyed "Indian," Lucullus Virgil McWhorter, whom the Yakimas adopted many snows ago and named *He-mēne Kā'wan* (Old Wolf). His heart is warm toward the red people. In him the Indians of the Pacific Northwest have a true friend. But for his insistence and encouragement, these legends would not have been set down by me for the children of another race to read.

Mourning Dove.

CONTENTS

I
The Spirit Chief Names
the Animal People

I

THE SPIRIT CHIEF NAMES THE
ANIMAL PEOPLE

AH-AH' EEL-ME'-WHEM, the great Spirit Chief,[1] called the Animal People together. They came from all parts of the world. Then the Spirit Chief told them there was to be a change, that a new kind of people was coming to live on the earth.

"All of you *Chip-chap-tiqulk*—Animal People—must have names," the Spirit Chief said. "Some of you have names now, some of you haven't. But tomorrow all will have names that shall be kept by you and your descendants forever. In the morning, as the first light of day shows in the sky, come to my lodge and choose your names. The first to come may choose any name that he or she wants. The next person may

---

[1] *Hah-ah'*, or *Hwa-hwa'*—Spirit. *Eel-me'-whem*—Chief. While the Okanogan, Colville, and other Salishan stock tribes of the interior paid homage to a great variety of minor "powers" or deities (as many members of the tribes still do), they firmly believed in a Spirit Chief, or Chief Spirit, an all-powerful Man Above. This belief was theirs before they ever heard of Christianity, notwithstanding statements that have been made to the contrary.

take any other name. That is the way it will go until all the names are taken. And to each person I will give work to do."

That talk made the Animal People very excited. Each wanted a proud name and the power to rule some tribe or some part of the world, and everyone determined to get up early and hurry to the Spirit Chief's lodge.

Sin-ka-lip'—Coyote—boasted that no one would be ahead of him. He walked among the people and told them that, that he would be the first. Coyote did not like his name; he wanted another. Nobody respected his name, Imitator, but it fitted him. He was called *Sin-ka-lip'* because he liked to imitate people. He thought that he could do anything that other persons did, and he pretended to know everything. He would ask a question, and when the answer was given he would say:

"I knew that before. I did not have to be told."

Such smart talk did not make friends for Coyote. Nor did he make friends by the foolish things he did and the rude tricks he played on people.

"I shall have my choice of the three biggest names," he boasted. "Those names are: *Kee-lau-naw*, the Mountain Person—Grizzly Bear, who will rule the four-footed people; *Milka-noups*—

Eagle,[2] who will rule the birds, and *En-tee-tee-ueh*, the Good Swimmer—Salmon. Salmon will be the chief of all the fish that the New People use for food."

Coyote's twin brother, Fox, who at the next sun took the name *Why-ay'-looh*—Soft Fur, laughed. "Do not be so sure, *Sin-ka-lip'*," said Fox. "Maybe you will have to keep the name you have. People despise that name. No one wants it."

"I am tired of that name," Coyote said in an angry voice. "Let someone else carry it. Let some old person take it—someone who cannot win in war. I am going to be a great warrior. My smart brother, I will make you beg of me when I am called Grizzly Bear, Eagle, or Salmon."

"Your strong words mean nothing," scoffed Fox. "Better go to your *swool'-hu* (tepee) and get some sleep, or you will not wake up in time to choose any name."

Coyote stalked off to his tepee. He told him-

---

[2]*Milka-noups*—the "War Eagle," or "Man Eagle" (golden eagle), whose white plumes with black or brown tips are prized for decorative and ceremonial purposes, particularly for war bonnets and other headgear, dance bustles, coup sticks, and shields. The tail feathers of the bald eagle, *Pak-la-kin* (White-headed-bird) are not valued so highly. In the old days the use of eagle feathers was restricted to the men. Except in rare instances, women were not privileged to wear them.

self that he would not sleep any that night; he would stay wide awake. He entered the lodge, and his three sons called as if with one voice:

"*Le-ee'-oo!*" ("Father!")³ [3]

They were hungry, but Coyote had brought them nothing to eat. Their mother, who after the naming day was known as *Pul'-laqu-whu*— Mole, the Mound Digger—sat on her foot at one side of the doorway. Mole was a good woman, always loyal to her husband in spite of his mean ways, his mischief-making, and his foolishness. She never was jealous, never talked back, never replied to his words of abuse. She looked up and said:

"Have you no food for the children? They are starving. I can find no roots to dig."

"*Eh-ha!*" Coyote grunted. "I am no common person to be addressed in that manner. I am going to be a great chief tomorrow. Did you know that? I will have a new name. I will be Grizzly Bear. Then I can devour my enemies with ease. And I shall need you no longer. You are growing too old and homely to be the wife of a great warrior and chief."

Mole said nothing. She turned to her corner of the lodge and collected a few old bones, which

---

³*Le-ee'-oo.* This form of address is employed only by males. A daughter calls her father *Mes-tem*, and her mother *Toom*. A son calls his mother *Se-go-ee*.

she put into a *klek'-chin* (cooking-basket).
With two sticks she lifted hot stones from the
fire and dropped them into the basket. Soon the
water boiled, and there was weak soup for the
hungry children.

"Gather plenty of wood for the fire," Coyote
ordered. "I am going to sit up all night."

Mole obeyed. Then she and the children went
to bed.

Coyote sat watching the fire. Half of the
night passed. He got sleepy. His eyes grew
heavy. So he picked up two little sticks and
braced his eyelids apart. "Now I can stay
awake," he thought, but before long he was fast
asleep, although his eyes were wide open.

The sun was high in the sky when Coyote
awoke. But for Mole he would not have wakened
then. Mole called him. She called him after she
returned with her name from the Spirit Chief's
lodge. Mole loved her husband. She did not
want him to have a big name and be a powerful
chief. For then, she feared, he would leave her.
That was why she did not arouse him at day-
break. Of this she said nothing.

Only half-awake and thinking it was early
morning, Coyote jumped at the sound of Mole's
voice and ran to the lodge of the Spirit Chief.
None of the other *Chip-chap-tiqulk* were there.
Coyote laughed. Blinking his sleepy eyes, he

walked into the lodge. "I am going to be *Kee-lau-naw*," he announced in a strong voice. "That shall be my name."

"The name Grizzly Bear was taken at dawn," the Spirit Chief answered.

"Then I shall be *Milka-noups*," said Coyote, and his voice was not so loud.

"Eagle flew away at sunup," the other replied.

"Well, I shall be called *En-tee-tee-ueh*," Coyote said in a voice that was not loud at all.

"The name Salmon also has been taken," explained the Spirit Chief. "All the names except your own have been taken. No one wished to steal your name."

Poor Coyote's knees grew weak. He sank down beside the fire that blazed in the great tepee, and the heart of *Hah-ah' Eel-me'-whem* was touched.

"*Sin-ka-lip'*," said that Person, "you must keep your name. It is a good name for you. You slept long because I wanted you to be the last one here. I have important work for you, much for you to do before the New People come. You are to be chief of all the tribes.

"Many bad creatures inhabit the earth. They bother and kill people, and the tribes cannot increase as I wish. These *En-alt-na Skil-ten*— People-Devouring Monsters—cannot keep on like that. They must be stopped. It is for you to conquer them. For doing that, for all the good things you do, you will be honored and praised by the people that are here now and that come afterward. But, for the foolish and mean things you do, you will be laughed at and despised. That you cannot help. It is your way.

"To make your work easier, I give you *squastenk'*. It is your own special magic power. No one else ever shall have it. When you are in danger, whenever you need help, call to your power. It will do much for you, and with it you can change yourself into any form, into anything you wish.

"To your twin brother, *Why-ay'-looh,* and to others I have given *shoo'-mesh.*[4] It is strong power. With that power Fox can restore your life should you be killed. Your bones may be scattered but, if there is one hair of your body left, Fox can make you live again. Others of the people can do the same with their *shoo'-mesh.* Now, go, *Sin-ka-lip'!* Do well the work laid for your trail!"

------

[4]*Shoo'-mesh.* With the exception of Coyote's "power," all "medicine" is spoken of as *shoo'-mesh,* which is regarded as definite aid communicated by the Spirit Chief through various mediums, inanimate objects as well as living creatures. Not infrequently an Indian will seek to test the potency of his medicine over that of another. Some present day medicine-men and medicine-women are reputed to possess magic power strong enough to cause the sickness or even the death of enemies, of anyone incurring their displeasure.

Well, Coyote was a chief after all, and he felt good again. After that day his eyes were different. They grew slant from being propped open that night while he sat by his fire. The New People, the Indians, got their slightly slant eyes from Coyote.

After Coyote had gone, the Spirit Chief thought it would be nice for the Animal People and the coming New People to have the benefit of the spiritual sweat-house. But all of the Animal People had names, and there was no one to take the name of Sweat-house—*Quil'-sten,* the Warmer.[5] So the wife of the Spirit

---

[5]*Quil'-sten*—Sweat-house. A mystic shrine for both temporal and spiritual cleansing, the sweat-house is one of the most venerated institutions. Its use is governed by strict rules, said to have originated with Coyote, the great "law-giver." To break any of the rules is to invite misfortune, if not disaster.

Sweat-houses, or lodges, are mound-shaped, round at the base, three and one-half to four feet high at the center, and four to six feet in diameter, accommodating three to five persons. In some sweat-houses there is room but for one or two bathers.

Willow shoots, service berry or other pliant stems, depending upon the locality and growth available, are planted like interlocking croquet wickets to make the frame. Where these "ribs" cross, they are tied together with strips of bark. There are never less than eight ribs. The frame is covered with swamp tule mats, blankets, or canvas. In primitive times sheets of cottonwood bark, top-dressed with earth, frequently formed the covering. Where a permanent residence is established, the framework is covered with tule mats, top-dressed with three or more inches of soil that is

Chief took the name. She wanted the people to have the sweat-house, for she pitied them. She wanted them to have a place to go to purify themselves, a place where they could pray for strength and good luck and strong medicine-power, and where they could fight sickness and get relief from their troubles.

The ribs, the frame poles, of the sweat-house represent the wife of *Hah-ah' Eel-me'-whem.* As she is a spirit, she cannot be seen, but she always is near. Songs to her are sung by the present generation. She hears them. She hears what her people say, and in her heart there is love and pity.

---

well packed and smoothed. The floor is carpeted with matting, grass, ferns, or fir boughs. The last are regarded as "strong medicine," and always are used if obtainable. They give the bather strength, and they are liked, besides, for their aromatic odor. The Indians rub their bodies with the soft tips of the fir boughs, both for the purpose of deriving power and for the scent imparted.

Just within and at one side of the lodge entrance, a small hole serves as a receptacle for the stones that are heated in a brisk fire a few steps from the structure. The stones, the size of a man's fist, are smooth, unchipped, "dry land" stones—never river-bed rocks. The latter crack and explode too easily when subjected to a combination of intense heat and cold water. By means of stout sticks, the heated stones are carried or rolled from the fire into the sweat-house. Then the entrance is curtained tightly with mat or blanket, and the bather sprinkles cold water on the little pile of stones, creating a dense steam.

To the novice, five minutes spent in the sweltering, midnight blackness of the cramping structure seem an eternity and almost unendurable.

Several "sweats," each followed by a dip in a nearby stream or pool, properly constitute one sweat-bath. The customary period for a single sweat is ten to twenty minutes, although votaries from rival bands or tribes often crouch together in the steam for twice or thrice that time. Thus they display to one another their virility and hardihood. To further show their strength and their contempt for the discomfort of such protracted sweating, they will blow on their arms and chests. The forcing of the breath against the superheated skin produces a painful, burning sensation. Hours, even days, may be spent in "sweat-housing."

The stones used are saved and piled outside the sweat-lodge, where they remain undisturbed. For services rendered they are held in a regard bordering on reverence. An Indian would not think of spitting or stepping on these stones or of "desecrating" them in any way.

Old-time warriors and hunters always "sweat-housed" before starting on their expeditions, and many of the modern, school-educated Indian men and women often resort to the sweat-house to pray for good fortune and health.

II
Fox and Coyote
and Whale

FOX AND COYOTE AND WHALE

FOX HAD a beautiful wife. He was very much in love with her, but she had stopped caring for him. Fox was a great hunter, and every day he brought home food and fine skins for his wife to make into robes and clothing. He did not know that, while he was away hunting, his wife would sit beside the *Swah-netk'-qhu*[1] and sing love songs to the water. Painting her face with bright colors, she would pour out her love thoughts in song.

Coyote came to visit his twin brother, and he soon noticed the strange actions of his sister-in-law. He spoke to Fox. "*Why-ay'-looh*," he said, "I think your wife is in love with somebody else." But Fox could not believe she loved anyone but him. He was blinded by his love for her. Then, one sun, he and Coyote returned from a hunt and she was not in the lodge. So Fox started to look for her. He walked down toward the river

---

[1]*Swah-netk'-qhu* (also recorded as *Swah-netk'-qha, Swah-netk'-qua, Soin-et'-kwu* and *Schwan-ate'-koo*—the Columbia River).

and there he saw his wife. She was sitting on the river bank, singing a love song. She did not see Fox. He watched her.

As Fox watched, the water began to rise. Slowly it rose, higher and higher, and soon, out in the middle of the river, appeared a big monster of the fish-kind. The monster was *En-hah-et'-qhu*, the Spirit of the Water—Whale. It swam to the shore. As it touched dry land, it changed into a tall handsome man with long braided hair. This monster-man made love to the wife of Fox.

Sad at heart, Fox turned away. He went to his lodge. He said nothing, but he wondered how he could win back his wife's love. He worried about her as the suns passed. She grew pale and thin. Nothing that Fox could do pleased her. Her thoughts always were with the man who was not a man but a monster. One day when Fox and Coyote came home from hunting, she was gone, and the fire in the lodge was cold. Fox called and called. He got no answer. His heart was heavy.

A few suns later Fox looked up the river and saw an odd-shaped canoe coming. It was only half of a canoe. Two Water Maidens were standing in it, rocking it from side to side. They were singing:

We come for food,
Food for the Chief's stolen wife.
The water-food does not suit her.
That is why we come! We come!

As the Water Maidens approached, Fox and Coyote hid in the tepee. The maidens beached the half-canoe and entered the lodge. They began to pick up dried meat to take to the stolen wife. Coyote and Fox sprang from their hiding places and caught the maidens, and Fox asked about his wife—where she was and how to get to her. The maidens were silent. Then the brothers threatened to kill them unless they answered, and the maidens said:

"To find the person who stole her, you must go over the Big Falls[2] and under the water. His

---

[2]Big Falls—Kettle Falls in the Columbia River, two miles below the mouth of Kettle River, in Stevens and Ferry counties, Washington. *Swah-netk'-qhu,* which means "Big Water" and also "Big Waterfalls," is applied by the Okanogan to Kettle Falls, as well as to the river. Early French-Canadian travelers, trappers and traders called the falls *La Chaudiere,* hence "Kettle." The water churning in the pot-holes among the rocks was likened to water boiling in huge kettles or caldrons. The Indians call these pot-holes *klek'-chin* because of their fancied resemblance to the primitive cooking-baskets. For many years prior to the establishment of Fort Colville, and even thereafter, the Indians living in the vicinity of the falls were known as *Les Chaudieres* and as Kettle, Bucket, Caldron, and Pot Indians.

lodge is under the falls, under the water—a dangerous trip for Land People. Every trail is watched. Even if you get there, the mighty Whale chief will kill you. He is bad."

The Water Maidens had told all they knew, so Fox broke their necks. He and Coyote dressed in the maidens' robes and started down the river in the half-canoe. Standing on the sides of the strange craft, they rocked it as they had seen the maidens do, and rode it down the river and over the roaring falls. "Let me do all the talking," Fox warned Coyote. "I know better what to say." Down through the pouring, flashing waters they shot with the half-canoe. The thunder of the falls hurt their ears. And then, suddenly, they were landing at a great encampment of Water People, a strange kind of people to them. All of the people were strange except *Gou-kouh-whay'-na*—Mouse. She was there. She knew them and they knew her. Fox jumped ashore. Coyote, following, tripped and touched the water, and Mouse, the Sly One, laughed. "Ha-ha!" said Mouse, "Coyote nearly fell into the water."

"Do not speak," Fox whispered to Mouse. "Say nothing. I will pay you well."

But some of the Water People had heard. "What, *Gou-kouh-whay'-na*, did you say?" they inquired.

"Nothing," Mouse answered. "Nothing of importance. I was just joking."

"Yes, you did say something," said a Water Person. "You said that Coyote nearly fell into the water. You cannot fool me."

Mouse insisted that she had not said that, and the other Water People believed her. They knew she was a fickle person and giddy, and they did not think much of her because she went everywhere to steal. She went everywhere, and that is why she understood all the different languages.

Carrying packs of dried meat and berries they had brought with them, Coyote and Fox made their way to the lodge of Whale, the chief. He and the stolen wife sat side by side in the lodge. The wife was glad to get the meat and berries, her kind of food.

Fox and Coyote kept their robes over their faces until everyone else was asleep. Then, when everything was quiet, Fox slipped up to Whale and cut off the monster's head with a flint knife. At the same time Coyote picked up the stolen wife and ran for the broken canoe. The noise they made awoke the camp, and the people rushed out of their lodges to see Coyote carrying off Fox's wife and Fox close behind, carrying the head of their chief. The people chased them, but the three got into the broken canoe, and Fox quickly put Coyote and the woman into his *shoo'-mesh* pipe. Then Fox pushed the half-canoe into the water and it shot up to the river's surface below the falls. There Fox landed. He took Coyote and his twice-stolen wife out of the medicine-pipe, and the head of the Whale Monster he threw toward the setting sun.

"In the Big Salt Water (ocean) shall Whale Monster stay," said Fox. "No longer shall he live in the smaller waters, in the rivers, where he can make love to the wives of men, where he can lure wives from their husbands."

As Fox and his wife and brother walked up the bank to their tepee, the headless body of Whale Monster turned over and over in the depths of the river, making the Big Falls of the *Swah-netk'-qhu* more fearful and thunderous, the way they are today, spilling with such force over the great rocks.

The wife of Fox became contented and happy again, glad to be back in her husband's lodge. But since that day Whale Monster was vanquished the Land People and the Water People have not loved each other. Fox made it so.

III
Coyote Fights Some Monsters

III

COYOTE FIGHTS SOME MONSTERS

COYOTE was far from his home by the *Swah-nekt'-qhu*. For many suns he had been traveling toward the sunrise. He had crossed the Rocky Mountains and was in the great plains country. *Sin-kit-zas-caw'-ha* — Horse — lived there. Horse was a dangerous monster, and he was much bigger than is any horse today.

As soon as he saw Coyote, Horse took after him. They ran and ran over the bare plains. Every time that Coyote looked back, Horse was closer. Coyote became scared. "*Squas-tenk'!*" he cried. "Do something for me!"

His power heard. It made three trees. They grew out of the ground straight ahead of him. And just in time, for Horse was about to catch him.

Into the first tree jumped Coyote. He laughed, for he thought he was safe. But his laugh was short; Horse began to cut down the tree with his strong teeth and great hoofs. Horse made the splinters fly. Soon the tree creaked, and then it cracked and groaned, and then—*shee-wha-a-am!*—it crashed to the plain, and Coyote went sailing through the air. He hit the ground hard, and Horse thought he had him, but Coyote staggered to his feet and got into the second tree.

Then Horse cut down that tree, and Coyote had another bad fall. Horse almost caught him. But Coyote skipped and dodged and finally got into the third tree. "Now what can I do?" he wondered. He was in a bad fix. Horse began to chop this last tree out from under him.

"Oh, *Sin-kit-zas-caw'-ha*, wait!" Coyote shouted. "I am not ready to die. Before you kill me, let me smoke my pipe—my pipe I like so well."

"You may have one smoke, *Sin-ka-lip'*," said Horse. "That is all. After that I shall kill you."

Puffing on his pipe, Coyote spoke to his medicine. It gave him a whip. Coyote jumped on his enemy's broad back, and struck fiercely with the whip. Horse was taken by surprise. He bawled and bucked; he whirled around and around; he stood on his hind feet and on his front feet; he threw himself; he rolled—tried all his tricks.

Coyote stayed with him, and he kept smacking Horse with the medicine-whip. He whipped Horse until the monster's head was battered and his eyes were swollen shut. After awhile Horse could not buck and fight any more. He was tired out. He begged for mercy. Coyote hopped off his back and looked at him. Horse was changed. He was not big and dangerous now. He was smaller, much smaller. Coyote had beaten him down.

"From this sun you are for people to ride," Coyote said. "Only when first ridden will you buck and be mean. Even old men will be able to sit on you. And old women will use you for carrying their camp things. On you they will put their heavy packs of roots and berries and meat."

He left the horse standing there, and went on. His way led past a cave. It was the home of *Kika-wau'-pa*—Dog who was a big and ferocious monster. Dog rushed out of the cave. Coyote ran. Coyote stumbled, falling into a mole hole, and that made him think of his faithful wife, Mole. Making himself small, he crawled into the hole, and there was Mole herself.

"Make your underground trails," Coyote said. "Make many of your tunnels. Hurry!"

Mole set to work. She dug fast, for Dog was digging to get at her husband. She dug many tunnels, as Coyote had ordered.

Dog soon uncovered Coyote, who then resumed his usual form, and said:

"Wait, *Kika-wau'-pa!* Do not kill me yet. Let me smoke my pipe first."

Dog did not object to that, and Coyote smoked. As he sucked on his pipe, Coyote spoke to his *squas-tenk'*. It gave him an armful of stones. Hitting Dog with a stone, he ran. Dog howled with pain and rage, and set out after him. Dog stumbled over one of Mole's mounded tunnels and fell, and Coyote hit him with another stone. Dog did not know that Mole had been busy changing the ground there, and every time he came to a tunnel he stumbled and fell, and each time he went down Coyote hit him with a stone. That was the way it went, and in a little while Dog was so tired and bruised that he could not take another step. Then Coyote finished him, and out of the monster's body ran a small dog, its tail between its legs.

"You shall be the most faithful animal the New People will have," said Coyote to the little dog. "Even old men and old women will own you. You will both fear and like your owners. Never must you attack a stranger unless the stranger treats you badly."

Coyote left the little dog. Presently he came to a big *che-yeep'* (tree), which he started to pass around. The tree bent and caught him with its branches. He wriggled and squirmed, but he could not get loose, so he whispered to his medicine. At once a great strength came to Coyote. With a mighty wrench, he tore the tree apart; tore it into two forks, like unfinished canoes, and he was free. Looking around, he noticed on the ground the bleached bones of travelers whom Tree Monster had eaten, and he said:

"After this sun you cannot hurt anyone. No one will fear you. You will provide wood for the New People. Because your limbs are pitchy and so easy to burn, all trees that are forked will be the kind that the old women will go to for firewood. That wood will be easy for them to gather."

From that place Coyote's trail took him into a deep *insis-k-chin* (canyon). As he walked deeper and deeper into it, he felt himself being swallowed. Scared, he tried to turn back. He could not move. He begged not to be eaten. The sound of his voice made Canyon Monster hesitate, and Coyote spoke to his *squas-tenk'*. It placed a long tree on his shoulders. Coyote swung the tree across the mouth of Canyon Monster. Then he laughed—the monster could not hurt him now.

"You no longer are a person-eating monster," Coyote said. "The New People will not be afraid of you. When they are too lazy to walk down your throat, they will walk on trees thrown across your mouth."

Coyote walked away from there and came to a coulee. He started into it. Something bumped and pricked his back. He could not see anything behind him and he ran. But the strange jabbing and bumping did not stop, so he stood still and spoke to his power. It gave him a flint knife. He slashed back over his shoulder. The knife struck something solid, and there was a loud groan and a heavy thud. Then Coyote saw what had been bothering him. On the ground was *Ste-eel'-tza*— Elk.[1] That monster was dead. Its power to stay invisible was gone. Coyote made a small elk from Elk Monster's body.

"No more shall you abuse people on the trails," he said. "You will fear the New People, and they will use your flesh for food and your skin for robes."

Coyote went on. He saw a cradleboard propped against a tree. Fastened in the cradle was a baby. No one else was in sight, and Coyote wondered where the mother had gone. Hoping he might be paid for showing attention to the little one, Coyote rocked it and sang. He wanted

---

[1]*Ste-eel'-tza*—"pounded-meat." As the fresh elk meat tends to spoil quickly, most of it is "jerked," or dried, or made into pemmican. When half dry, the meat is pounded to break the fibre, which makes it easier to chew.

If made into pemmican, the meat is mixed with grease and service berries. Properly prepared, pemmican will keep for several years.

In the old days, much of this jerked elk meat and elk pemmican was obtained by the Okanogans in trade. It was transported from the source of supply and from camp to camp in rawhide containers, parfleches, which the Indians called *pen'-pen-nox* (folded-at-the-ends).

the mother to hear and come. Louder and louder he sang, but nobody came, and the baby began to cry. Thinking it must be hungry, Coyote poked one of his fingers into its mouth. "Do not cry," he said. "Here is *tah-tat!*"

Then Coyote had a surprise. The baby was swallowing his hand! He jerked his hand away; the flesh was stripped off clean. Coyote realized that he was holding, not a baby, but a person-eating monster.

"I will find your mother, little *skwas-qu-see* (baby). I will look for her," he said, and he put the baby down and walked away. He slipped into a thicket. There he called softly to his *squas-tenk'*. It handed him a flint knife that was shaped like a finger. The blade was sharp. Coyote returned to Baby Monster and picked it up. Talking nice words, he put the knife-finger in the monster's mouth. He held the knife-finger in his own fingers, and Baby Monster swallowed his whole arm. That was what Coyote wanted. He pulled his arm back, pulled it back quickly, and the sharp knife-finger ripped open the monster's insides. Out tumbled a lot of bones, bones of people the false baby had eaten.

"You cannot do this way any more," said Coyote. "A New People soon will be here. You are not to eat them as you have these others. From now on, babies, when born, will be the most helpless of all creatures. That must be, so you cannot cheat by taking their form."

Weary of fighting monsters, Coyote started for home. "Even babies are monsters in this strange land," he remarked. "I will go back to my own country by the *Swah-netk'-qhu* and rest."

IV
Chipmunk and Owl-Woman

I V

CHIPMUNK AND OWL-WOMAN

K*OTS-SE-WE-AH* — Chipmunk —was a little girl. She lived with her grandmother in the woods. Chipmunk liked to walk through the woods and pick berries. Some of the berries she ate, and some she put in a little basket that hung at her side. The basket was made from a deer's hoof.

There was one berry bush that the little girl visited every day. She called it her very own. It was a *see'-ah* (service berry) bush.[1] She would climb into it and eat all the berries she could hold. And as she ate them she would count: "One berry ripe! Two berries ripe! Three berries ripe!"

One sun, while in the bush counting and eating berries, Chipmunk heard steps on the ground below. She looked. Standing under the bush was *Snee'-nah*—Owl-woman. On Owl-woman's

---

[1]The service berry, *Amelanchier alnifolia*. The fruit resembles the black currant but has a sweeter flavor. The Indians gather large quantities and sun-dry them for winter use. The berries are used also in the making of pemmican.

back was a big basket, and in the basket were many little children that Owl-woman had stolen. Owl-woman traveled from camp to camp, stealing children. Whenever she got hungry she ate one or two of them.

Chipmunk was not frightened very much, for she knew that Owl-woman could not reach her up in the *see'-ah* bush, and Owl-woman knew that too. But Owl-woman was cunning. In her best voice, she said: "*Kots-se-we-ah*, your father wants you."

"I have no father," Chipmunk answered. "He died long ago."

Owl-woman thought for a moment. Then she said: "Your mother wants you. She wants you to come home."

"My mother died many snows ago," Chipmunk replied.

"Your aunt wants you to come home."

"I never had an aunt," and Chipmunk laughed.

"Your uncle is looking for you," lied Owl-woman.

"That is funny," said Chipmunk, laughing some more. "I never had an uncle."

"Well," Owl-woman sighed, "your grandfather wants you."

"That is strange, for my grandfather died before I was born."

Then Owl-woman said: "Your grandmother wants you at home right away!"

Chipmunk could believe that. She was silent for a little, and then she said:

"I will not come down unless you hide your eyes."

"All right, I will hide my eyes. See! I have them covered," and Owl-woman pretended that she had. She placed her claw-hands over them.

"I can see your big eyes blinking behind your fingers," cried Chipmunk. "I shall not come down until you have hidden them entirely."

Owl-woman pretended to hide her eyes entirely, but she left a small space between her fingers—just a little crack to look through.

Chipmunk really thought that the eyes were covered, but she wasn't taking any chance of being fooled. Instead of dropping from branch to branch to the ground, she jumped from the top of the bush. She jumped over Owl-woman's head, and, as she went sailing over, Owl-woman reached for her. Owl-woman's fingers clawed down Chipmunk's back, ripping off long strips of the soft fur, but the little girl got away. Ever since that time the chipmunks have carried the marks of Owl-woman's claws—the marks are the stripes you see on the chipmunks' backs.

Chipmunk ran and ran, and Owl-woman followed as fast as she could.

When Chipmunk reached home, she was trembling and out of breath. She hardly could speak. All she could say was:

"*Sing-naw! Sing-naw!*" ("Owl! Owl!")

The deaf old grandmother misunderstood. "Did you step on a thorn?" she asked.

"*Sing-naw! Sing-naw!*" Chipmunk kept repeating. She was so frightened, it was all she could say.

Only after Chipmunk had said that many times did the grandmother understand. Then she tried to hide the little girl in her bed, but Chipmunk would not keep still there. She ran around under the robes. Anyone could see she was there. So the grandmother took her out of the bed and dropped her into a berry basket. But that wouldn't do, for Chipmunk rattled around in the basket and made a lot of noise. Then the grandmother tried to hide her in a basket of soup, and poor Chipmunk nearly drowned. She and her grandmother were in despair. They did not know what to do. Then they heard a voice—it came from a tree near the tepee. It was the voice of *Wy-wetz'-kula,* the Tattler—Meadow Lark, who was singing:

> "*Two little oyster shells
> Hide her in!*"

Quickly the grandmother put Chipmunk between two little oyster shells. And, knowing Meadow Lark was a gossip and a tattler, she took off her necklace and threw it to the singer. She hoped that the present would please Meadow Lark and keep her from telling where Chipmunk was hidden. Meadow Lark put on the necklace and flew away.

Soon Owl-woman came along.

"Where is the child I am hunting?" she said.

The grandmother pretended that she had not seen her grandchild, so Owl-woman began to look around. She looked in the bed, in the berry basket and in the soup. She looked everywhere she could think might be a hiding place. At last she turned to leave, and just then Meadow Lark flew back to the tree near the tepee. Meadow Lark sang:

> *"I will tell you, if you pay me.*
> *I will tell you, if you pay me.*
> *Where she is! Where she is!"*

Owl-woman hurried outside and threw a bright yellow vest to the Tattler, who put it on, and sang:

> *"Two little oyster shells,*
> *Take her out!*
> *Two little oyster shells,*
> *Take her out!"*

Then Meadow Lark flew away. The necklace she was given for helping Chipmunk and the yellow vest she earned for tattling she wears to this day.

Owl-woman pushed the grandmother aside and snatched Chipmunk out of the oyster shells. With her sharp fingers she cut Chipmunk open and took out her heart and swallowed it.

"*Eh!* Yom-yom! It is good. Little girls' hearts are the best," said Owl-woman, smacking her lips.

Owl-woman went her way, carrying her big basket of children. In a little while the weeping grandmother heard a familiar voice. Meadow Lark was singing again from the tree. Her song was:

> *"Put a berry in her heart!*
> *Put a berry in her heart!"*

Drying her tears, the grandmother put a half-ripe *see'-ah* berry in Chipmunk's breast and sewed up the hole. Then she stepped over Chipmunk three times, and Chipmunk jumped up as alive and as well as ever.

Owl-woman had not walked far when she met Coyote. He knew her—knew how wicked she was. "*Snee'-nah*," he said, "I like to eat children, too. Let us travel together and we will have better luck finding them."

Owl-woman was pleased. She thought that the two of them, traveling together and helping each other, would be stronger than all of the monsters in the world. She smiled. "Yes, that is good," she said. "Let us go together." So they walked along like old friends.

Pretty soon Coyote said: "I am getting hungry. Here is a good place to make a fire. Let us stop here and roast those children you are carrying in the basket."

Owl-woman said she was hungry, too, and she set her big basket on the ground. Coyote persuaded her to let all of the children out so they could do the work of gathering wood for the fire. Coyote bossed them around, talking in a cruel way. That was for Owl-woman's ears— that cruel talk. But to each child he whispered: "Get the wood that has the most pitch and get plenty of solid pitch. Do that if you wish to return to your parents."

Coyote's words made the children work hard. Soon there was a roaring fire.

"This is to be an important feast," Coyote told Owl-woman. "You should paint your face. Paint it with charcoal and rub it with pitch. The pitch will make the charcoal stay on. Your arms should be painted the same way. The children and I will help you fix up."

Coyote's attention flattered Owl-woman. She

let him and the children help her to prepare for the feast. They painted her arms with charcoal, and then smeared them with pitch, and she painted her face the same way.

"Now, let us roast the children," she said.

"No, not yet," Coyote advised. "Wait until the wood burns to red coals. That pitch smoke would spoil the taste. But we can do something while we are waiting. We can dance. Let us dance the Sun-dance. While we are having a good time, the children shall gather forked roasting sticks."

"Good, we will dance," said Owl-woman. "But why the forked roasting sticks?"

"Because forked sticks are better than straight ones for roasting children."

Coyote told the children to hurry and gather forked sticks, and he and Owl-woman began to dance. They danced and danced. Owl-woman grew tired. She wanted to stop.

"Do not stop so soon," Coyote urged. "You are a good dancer. I like to see you dance."

Owl-woman believed those sly words. She danced harder and harder, until she staggered. Then, as if in play, Coyote shoved her, and she fell. Coyote laughed, and Owl-woman laughed, and she got up and danced again. Coyote danced beside her. And when she got close to the fire he shoved her right into the flames. He called to the children, and they brought the forked sticks which they and Coyote used to hold Owl-woman in the fire. Covered as she was with pitch, Owl-woman burned like pitchwood.

In that way perished the wicked Owl-woman. Bad persons always must pay for the evil workings of their minds.

V

Coyote and the Buffalo

V

COYOTE AND THE BUFFALO

NO BUFFALO ever lived in the *Swah-netk'-qhu* country. That was Coyote's fault. If he had not been so foolish and greedy, the people beside the *Swah-netk'-qhu* would not have had to cross the Rockies to hunt the *quas-peet-za* (curled-hairs).[1]

This is the way it happened:

Coyote was traveling over the plains beyond the big mountains. He came to a flat. There he found an old buffalo skull. It was the skull of Buffalo Bull. Coyote always had been afraid of Buffalo Bull. He remembered the many times Bull Buffalo had scared him, and he laughed upon seeing the old skull there on the flat.

"Now I will have some fun," Coyote remarked. "I will have revenge for the times Buffalo made me run."

He picked up the skull and threw it into the

---

[1]*Quas-peet-za* ("curled-hairs" or "curly-haired.") The same word is used for "buffalo robes." The Okanogan and other interior Northwest tribes occasionally hunted buffalo east of the Rockies, and they frequently obtained buffalo robes and dried buffalo meat in trade.

air; he kicked it and spat on it; he threw dust in the eye-sockets. He did these things many times, until he grew tired. Then he went his way. Soon he heard a rumbling behind him. He thought it was thunder, and he looked at the sky. The sky was clear. Thinking he must have imagined the sound, he walked on, singing. He heard the rumbling again, only much closer and louder. Turning around, he saw Buffalo Bull pounding along after him, chasing him. His old enemy had come to life!

Coyote ran, faster than he thought he could run, but Buffalo gained steadily. Soon Buffalo was right at his heels. Coyote felt his hot breath.

"Oh, *Squas-tenk'*, help me!" Coyote begged, and his power answered by putting three trees in front of him. They were there in the wink of an eye. Coyote jumped and caught a branch of the first tree and swung out of Buffalo's way. Buffalo rammed the tree hard, and it shook as if in a strong wind. Then Buffalo chopped at the trunk with his horns, first with one horn and then the other. He chopped fast, and in a little while over went the tree, and with it went Coyote. But he was up and into the second tree before Buffalo Bull could reach him. Buffalo soon laid that tree low, but he was not quick enough to catch Coyote, who scrambled into the third and last tree.

"Buffalo, my friend, let me talk with you,"

said Coyote, as his enemy hacked away at the tree's trunk. "Let me smoke my pipe. I like the *kinnikinnick*.² Let me smoke. Then I can die more content."

"You may have time for one smoke," grunted Bull Buffalo, resting from his chopping.

Coyote spoke to his medicine-power, and a pipe, loaded and lighted, was given to him. He puffed on it once and held out the pipe to Buffalo Bull.

"No, I will not smoke with you," said that one. "You made fun of my bones. I have enough enemies without you. Young Buffalo is one of them. He killed me and stole all my fine herd."

"My uncle,"³ said Coyote, "you need new

---

²*Kinnikinnick*—the Bear Berry, *Arctostaphylos Uvaursi*, which grows on high mountain ridges. The thick evergreen leaves are toasted and then crumbled. The modern mixture for pipe smoking is about two-thirds tobacco to one-third *kinnikinnick*. The leaves are toasted either before an open fire, by placing a sprig of the plant in a cleft stick that is stuck in the ground, or in a sweat-house. In the latter case, branches of the shrub are laid on the sweat-house framework, between the frame and the covering, and left for an hour or more—during the course of a sweat-bath. The leaves are browned and dried as effectively by the steam as by dry heat.

³"My uncle." Coyote is not claiming actual relationship with Buffalo. He uses the term to curry favor. Indians commonly employ *uncle, cousin, brother, sister, aunt, grandfather* and *grandmother* in addressing persons to whom they are not related. They do this either to express genuine affection or respect, or to cajole and flatter. Cousins and intimate friends regularly are called *brothers* or *sisters*.

horns. Let me make new horns for you. Then you can kill Young Buffalo. Those old horns are dull and worn."

Bull Buffalo was pleased with that talk. He decided he did not want to kill Coyote. He told Coyote to get down out of the tree and make the new horns. Coyote jumped down and called to his power. It scolded him for getting into trouble, but it gave him a flint knife and a stump of pitchwood. From this stump Coyote carved a pair of fine heavy horns with sharp points. He gave them to Buffalo Bull. All buffalo bulls have worn the same kind of horns since.

Buffalo Bull was very proud of his new horns. He liked their sharpness and weight and their pitch-black color. He tried them out on what was left of the pitchwood stump. He made one toss and the stump flew high in the air, and he forgave Coyote for his mischief. They became good friends right there. Coyote said he would go along with Buffalo Bull to find Young Buffalo.

They soon came upon Young Buffalo and the big herd he had won from Buffalo Bull. Young Buffalo laughed when he saw his old enemy, and he walked out to meet him. He did not know, of course, about the new horns. It was not much of a fight, that fight between Young Buffalo and Buffalo Bull. With the fine new horns, Buffalo Bull killed the other easily, and then he took back his herd, all his former wives and their children. He gave Coyote a young cow, the youngest cow, and he said:

"Never kill her, *Sin-ka-lip'!* Take good care of her and she will supply you with meat forever. When you get hungry, just slice off some choice fat with a flint knife. Then rub ashes on the wound and the cut will heal at once."

Coyote promised to remember that, and they parted. Coyote started back to his own country, and the cow followed. For a few suns he ate only the fat when he was hungry. But after awhile he became tired of eating fat, and he began to long for the sweet marrow-bones and the other good parts of the buffalo. He smacked his lips at the thought of having some warm liver.

"Buffalo Bull will never know," Coyote told himself, and he took his young cow down beside a creek and killed her.

As he peeled off the hide, crows and magpies came from all directions. They settled on the carcass and picked at the meat. Coyote tried to chase them away, but there were too many of them. While he was chasing some, others returned and ate the meat. It was not long until they had devoured every bit of the meat.

"Well, I can get some good from the bones and marrow-fat," Coyote remarked, and he built a fire to cook the bones. Then he saw an old woman walking toward him. She came up to the fire.

"*Sin-ka-lip'*," she said, "you are a brave warrior, a great chief. Why should you do woman's work? Let me cook the bones while you rest."

Vain Coyote! He was flattered. He believed she spoke her true mind. He stretched out to rest and he fell asleep. In his sleep he had a bad dream. It awoke him, and he saw the old woman running away with the marrow-fat and the boiled grease. He looked into the cooking-basket. There was not a drop of soup left in it. He chased the old woman. He would punish her! But she could run, too, and she easily kept ahead of him. Every once in awhile she stopped and held up the marrow-fat and shouted: "*Sin-ka-lip'*, do you want this?"

Finally Coyote gave up trying to catch her. He went back to get the bones. He thought he would boil them again. He found the bones scattered all around, so he gathered them up and put them into the cooking-basket. Needing some more water to boil them in, he went to the creek for it, and when he got back, there were no bones in the basket! In place of the bones was a little pile of tree limbs!

Coyote thought he might be able to get another cow from Buffalo Bull, so he set out to find him. When he came to the herd, he was astonished to see the cow he had killed. She was there with the others! She refused to go with Coyote again, and Buffalo Bull would not give him another cow. Coyote had to return to his own country without a buffalo.

That is why there never have been any buffalo along the *Swah-netk'-qhu.*

VI

Why the Flint-Rock Cannot Fight Back

VI
WHY THE FLINT-ROCK CANNOT FIGHT BACK

 *STO-WAY'-NA* — Flint[1] — was rich and powerful. His lodge was toward the sunrise. It was guarded by *Sqŭr-hein*—Crane. He was the watcher. He watched from the top of a lone tree. When anybody approached, Crane would call out and warn Flint, and Flint would come out of his lodge and meet the visitor.

There was an open flat in front of the lodge. Flint met all his visitors there. Warriors and hunters came and bought flint for arrow-points and spear-heads. They paid Flint big prices for the privilege of chipping off the hard stone. Some who needed flint for their weapons were poor and could not buy. These poor persons Flint turned away.

Coyote heard about Flint and, as he wanted some arrow-points, he asked his *squas-tenk'* to help him. *Squas-tenk'* refused.

"Hurry, do what I ask, or I will throw you away and let the rain wash you—wash you cold,"

[1]*Sto-way'-na*—literally "hard rock."

said Coyote, and then the power gave him three rocks that were harder than the flint-rock. It also gave him a little dog that had only one ear. But this ear was sharp, like a knife; it was a knife-ear.

Then to his wife, Mole, Coyote said: "Go and make your underground trails in the flat where *Sto-way'-na* lives. When you have finished and see me talking with him, show yourself so we can see you."

Then Coyote set out for Flint's lodge. As he got near it, he had his power make a fog to cover the land, and thick fog spread over everything. Crane, the watcher, up in the lone tree, could not see Coyote. He did not know that Coyote was around.

Coyote climbed the tree and took Crane from his high perch and broke his neck. Crane had no time to cry out. Then Coyote went on to Flint's lodge. He was almost there when Flint's dog, Grizzly Bear, jumped out of the lodge and ran toward him.

Coyote was not scared, and he yelled at Flint: "Stop your grizzly bear dog! Stop him, or my dog will kill him."

That amused Flint, who was looking through the doorway. He saw that Coyote's one-eared dog was very small, hardly a mouthful for Grizzly Bear. Flint came out of his lodge. He was laughing.

"*Sin-ka-lip'*, you better take your dog away. My Grizzly Bear will eat him up."

"No, stop your dog," repeated Coyote. "One-Ear is bad!"

"Hah!" laughed Flint. "No dog can hurt my Grizzly Bear!"

So, without more talk, Coyote sent One-Ear at Grizzly Bear, who opened his mouth wide. The little dog went right ahead and jumped straight into Grizzly Bear's mouth, and kept on going. He went clear through Grizzly Bear. His sharp knife-ear cut Flint's dog wide open.

"See!" Coyote said. "I told you that One-Ear was bad. He can kill anything."

About that time Mole appeared at the far edge of the flat. She was dressed in skins that were painted red, and she looked very handsome.

"My friend," Coyote spoke to Flint, "see that woman over there. Let us run a race. The one who gets to her first shall take her for his wife."

Flint was willing. So they raced. They ran toward Mole. She pretended to be digging *spit-lum* (bitter-root).[2] She had made tunnels all

---

[2]*Spit-lum* (bitter-root)—*Lewisia rediviva.* A small, slender, white starchy root that may be eaten raw but is preferred cooked. It is cooked by steaming or boiling. Many Indians today like it with cream and sugar, and it is relished when dried and mixed with huckleberries. It also is a favorite and effective remedy for digestive disturbances. The roots are peeled soon after they have been dug, before they have time to dry.

through the flat, and they were a bother to Flint. He kept stepping into them and falling, and every time he fell Coyote would jump over him, and shout: *"Eh! Ha-yea!* My friend, what is wrong?"

Flint was heavy, and slow in picking himself up. Sometimes Coyote jumped over him twice before he could get up. When they got to where Mole was standing, she changed herself into a real mole and skipped into one of her tunnels. Then Coyote began to hit Flint with the *squas-tenk'* rocks. At each blow they scaled off big flakes of flint.

Flint tried to catch Coyote, but every few steps he stumbled into one of Mole's tunnels, and he grew weaker and weaker. Coyote kept striking him with the medicine-rocks. At last all of the monster's body was chipped away. Only the heart was left. Then Flint died.

Coyote picked up the heart and threw it across the flat. There it is today. It is a hill standing there. Much flint is found there.[3]

---

[3]This hill, known as "Square Butte," is in Cascade County, Montana, twenty-two miles west and a little south of Great Falls, and about five miles south of the old Fort Shaw Indian School, which Mourning Dove attended for awhile in her girlhood. She frequently went to the butte with picnic parties of Indian children. Fairly flat on top with steep sides, the butte rises some four hundred feet above the surrounding plain, and can be seen from dis-

The pieces of Flint's body which were scattered around on the flat were gathered up by Coyote and thrown all over the earth for warriors and hunters to use.

That done, Coyote said: "*Sto-way'-na*, you are a person no more. From this sun you are only dead stone!"

And that is why the flint-rock is senseless and cannot fight back when chipped for arrow-heads. Coyote made it so before the New People came.

---

tances of thirty to forty miles in almost any direction. Old Indians say that flint of fine quality was to be found there. Columbia Basin Indians who ventured along the upper reaches of the Missouri River to hunt buffalo were familiar with the landmark. It was observed by the Lewis and Clark expedition on June 13, 1805, the same day on which Captain Lewis found the Great Falls of the Missouri.

The top of the butte is approximately two miles long in a direction a little northwest of north and south and about one and one-half miles wide, and is used for grazing purposes. It is said that there is only one point of access to the top; it is on the west side.

The butte wears a volcanic cap, the result of a volcanic overflow which occurred when the Mission Range, thirty miles to the south and about fifty miles long, east and west, was thrown up. The cap is pyroxene-porphyry, rather dense and roughly columnar, and rests on a sandstone formation which contains oyster shells and fine specimens of the straight baculite shell, perfectly preserved.

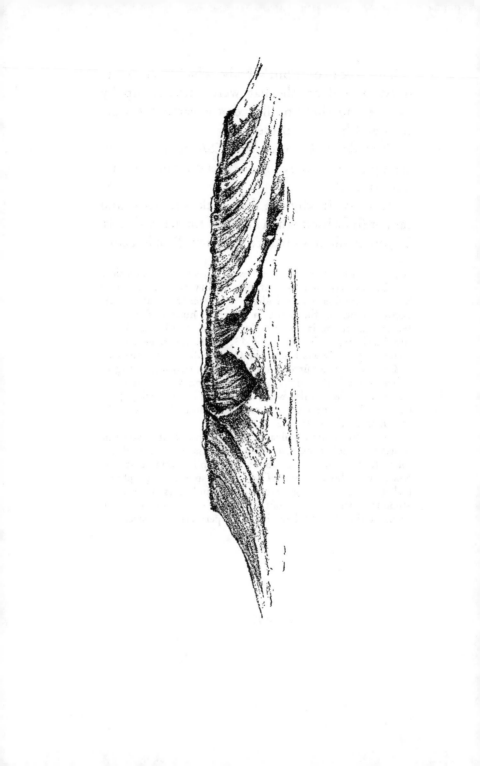

VII

How Turtle Got His Tail

VII

HOW TURTLE GOT HIS TAIL

 **N**O ONE could run faster than Rabbit. He had won many races and prizes. He had won Frog's tail from Frog and Bear's tail from Bear. Rabbit's own tail was very long.

One sun, Turtle, who had no tail at all, went to Rabbit and said: "*Spe-pa-lee'-na*, my friend, I would like to race with you. I think I can beat you. I would like to win those tails, yours and the others."

Rabbit laughed, for *Ar-sikh'* was such a slow traveler. Rabbit made fun of him before the people. But Turtle insisted, and Rabbit finally agreed to race with him. "Beating you will be easy," said Rabbit. "When do you want to race?"

"Let us race tomorrow while the morning is young," said Turtle.

The people all gathered the next morning early to watch the strange race between Rabbit, the swift-jumper, and Turtle, the slow-walker. They started, and Rabbit quickly left Turtle far behind.

"No use for me to run all the way now," Rabbit remarked to himself. "I will sit down awhile and wait for that silly *Ar-sikh'*. That will make him feel foolish." So Rabbit stopped to rest. He went to sleep. When he awoke, he was surprised to see Turtle moving slowly along some distance ahead.

"I must have slept long," said Rabbit, and he hopped swiftly after the slow-walker. He passed Turtle and kept on going until, when he looked back, he could not see the other. Then he sat down to wait, and again he fell asleep. While Rabbit slept, Turtle crawled by, and when Rabbit opened his eyes there was Turtle far ahead. But that did not worry Rabbit. He easily overtook the slow one.

That is the way they raced, Rabbit running and resting and going to sleep, and Turtle plodding, plodding without a stop. The race trail was long. It went to a half-way stake and returned to the point of starting. On the home stretch, Rabbit decided to take one last rest. He intended to stay awake, but, in spite of himself, he fell asleep. When he finally awoke he could not see Turtle anywhere.

"He ought to be in sight by now," said Rabbit. "Perhaps he has given up." Then Rabbit rubbed his eyes and looked again. Away off, near the finish-line, he saw a speck. It was Turtle.

Rabbit was startled. He jumped up and ran. He ran his fastest, but he had slept too long. Turtle crawled over the finish-line first. Rabbit was a few leaps behind. The people laughed and laughed at Rabbit, and he was very much ashamed.

Cutting off his own tail, so that there was only a little stump left, Rabbit gave it to Turtle. He also gave Turtle the other two tails. Turtle first tried on Bear's tail. It was too long and bushy. He threw it aside and tried on Rabbit's own tail. That did not suit him, either, as the fur was thick and fine—the water and mud would make it too heavy. Then Turtle put on Frog's tail.

"That is the tail I need," said Turtle. "Frog's tail matches my color, it hasn't any fur or hair on it, and it is just the right size."

All turtles have tails like that today, while rabbits have scarcely any tail at all.

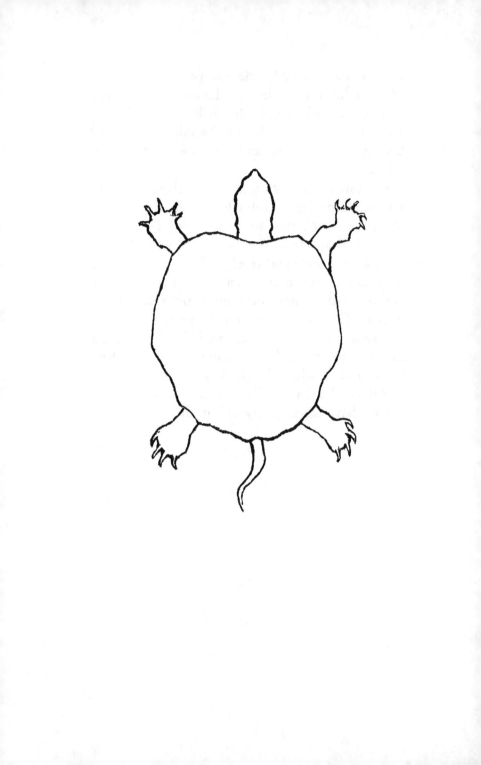

VIII

Why Skunk's Tail Is
Black and White

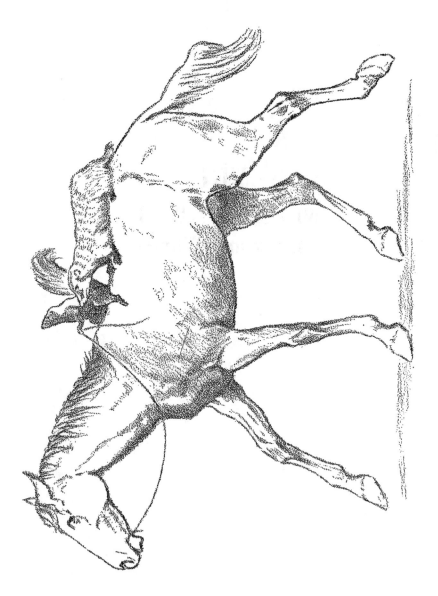

VIII

WHY SKUNK'S TAIL IS BLACK AND WHITE

 **F**AR OFF in his own country, *Sen-kes-tia* — Skunk — heard about the race between Turtle and Rabbit. As Skunk did not have a tail, he thought he would like to race Turtle for the tails of Rabbit and Bear. He set out for Turtle's country. With him went his friend, *E-whe-whoot'-ken*—Sharp-Claws. That was Badger. They rode a little white horse, and sat double, like warriors on parade.

When they got to where Turtle lived, Skunk asked him to race. Turtle refused. Skunk was very angry, for he had ridden a long way just to make that race, and he raised a big fuss. Now, the people were afraid of Skunk because of his strong odor; it was strong medicine. With it Skunk could kill people, and those persons there were afraid he might kill some of them. They told Turtle he had to race whether he wanted to or not. Then Turtle agreed, but Skunk said:

"I will not race on foot. My friend, *E-whe-whoot'-ken*, and I will ride double on this white horse."

"All right," Turtle replied, because he did not dare to object. "You ride the white horse."

Turtle knew he didn't have a chance in that race. It was over before he could even get a fair start, and he had to give the tails of Rabbit and Bear to Skunk. His own tail was safe. Skunk had no use for it.

Skunk put on both of the tails he had won. He made them into one tail, and that is why all skunks now have bushy black and white tails.

After the race Badger was not ready to go home. He wanted to stay and visit awhile, but Skunk made him get on the little white horse. They started. Pretty soon Badger thought of a trick to make Skunk leave him behind. Badger suddenly fell off the horse. He flopped off to the ground and pretended to be dead. Skunk got off and looked at him. Skunk felt very sad.

"I loved my friend, *E-whe-whoot'-ken*," Skunk cried. "I will not leave him in this place, so far from home. Rather than go away and leave him, I would eat him. Yes, I will eat him. I will eat him this evening."

Badger was scared. He had not thought of anything like that happening—of being eaten. He did not know what to do. Skunk cried and cried, and after awhile Skunk sang:

"I will never leave my friend, E-whe-whoot'-
ken.
I will not give up his flesh to anyone;
Not even to an enemy.
Only Whee'-Who—Whistler, the Hoary
Marmot—
Can make me run away and leave him."

That mention of Whistler, the Hoary Marmot, gave hope to Badger. He knew that Skunk was afraid of Whistler.

Skunk started to walk, carrying Badger in his arms. Badger whistled. It was a low whistle. Skunk jumped and looked around. Then Badger whistled a little louder. Skunk began to run. Badger whistled still louder, and Skunk threw him down and jumped into some thick brush. Skunk crawled deep into the brush to hide. He thought that Whistler was coming. Badger got up and ran, and Skunk did not see him go.

As Badger and Skunk parted as good friends, their friendship never has died.

IX

Rattlesnake and Salmon

IX

RATTLESNAKE AND SALMON

 **T**HE LODGE of *En-tee-tee-ueh*— Salmon—was in the cliffs above the Big Falls of the *Swah-netk'-qhu*. Salmon was a great warrior.

Salmon heard of a beautiful girl who lived in the Kalispel country. Many warriors were trying to win her, Salmon heard, and he decided he would win her himself. So he went to her country and made war on the people. He beat them and took away the maiden. He brought her home with him. She loved Salmon from the first. She loved him for his red handsome face.

Many warriors wanted to kill Salmon and take his bride, but they did not know how to get at the pair in the lodge above the roaring falls. But near Salmon's lodge lived *Hah-ah-ooh-lah*[1]—

---

[1]*Hah-ah-ooh-lah* (also pronounced *Hah-ah-lawh* and *Hwa-hwa-ulah*). Variously translated as: "Evil Spirit of the Earth," "Evil of the Earth," and "Wicked Crawler." Like the other interior Northwest tribes, the Okanogan believe that rattlesnakes have strong magic power, and they treat the reptiles with the utmost respect. Meeting a rattler, an Indian will address it with placating and ingratiat-

Rattlesnake. He was an old man. He envied Salmon. He decided to kill him. He made war-arrows, singing as he worked. And then, one sun when he had finished the arrows, Rattlesnake strung his bow and stepped outside his bough-covered lodge and sent an arrow into Salmon's head.

Salmon tumbled from his cliff home into the river. His body floated down the river. Salmon's wife cried. The three Wolf brothers had been watching. They saw Salmon die. They took Salmon's wife to their own camp. There she was made to work—to be a slave—and she was watched night and day by the wives of the three brothers. She was unhappy; she felt very bad.

The river carried Salmon's body a long way. Finally it was washed upon a sand-bar, to bleach in the sun. Soon only the skull and the back-bone remained.

Gou-kouh-whay'-na—Mouse, the Sly One—came there to the sand-bar one day with her sister. They were looking for something to steal.

---

ing words, to "keep on its good side." However much they may detest and dread the rattlesnake, they never talk about him save in a most respectful manner, because, they say, his power enables him to hear what is said, regardless of how far distant he may be from the speaker. And they will not kill a rattlesnake except as a matter of necessity—to save a life or ward off an attack—or for the sake of revenge, if the snake has attacked or injured someone.

They found what was left of Salmon. Mouse was very sad, for Salmon had been her chief. She went to a camp near-by and stole some salmon oil. With that oil she greased the skull and back-bone every sun for many suns. After awhile the flesh began to grow around the bones. Slowly Salmon was restored to life by the oil Mouse rubbed on him. At last he could get up and move around, and after many moons he became strong again. Then he went back to the Big Falls, to his home. As his wife was not there, he went over to Rattlesnake's lodge to ask about her. He heard Rattlesnake singing.

"Ta-pin-ee, ex-en-lee-ah!" ("I shot him, and he ran down the cliffs!")[2] And Rattlesnake sang this: "I shot him! He was a chief, but he is a chief no more!"

Salmon walked into Rattlesnake's lodge. Out of the corner of one eye, Rattlesnake saw him, but he did not let on that he saw, and he changed his song. He pretended to be mourning Salmon's death. Salmon said nothing. He stooped and picked a piece of blazing wood from the fire and touched it to the dry bough lodge covering. He jumped outside, and the flames leaped up. Rattlesnake was trapped. He could not get out; he was burned to death. From one of Rattle-

---

[2]The dialect here is not Okanogan. It is supposed to be Rattlesnake's own language.

snake's eyes crawled a small snake. It was Rattlesnake's mystery-power.

"Always shall you crawl on your belly," Salmon told the little rattlesnake. "That is my revenge."

Then Salmon started in search of his wife. He found her in the camp of the three Wolf brothers. Two of the brothers he killed, and he told the third, the youngest, to get out of that country. He told him to go into the timber country and never come back. Wolf went. He was the first of the timber wolves. That is how the race of timber wolves originated.

Salmon and his wife did not return to their lodge in the cliffs. He took her into the water below the Big Falls, where they would be safe from the enemies they had among the Land People.

The arrow-point that Rattlesnake shot into Salmon's head stayed in his head. All salmon have arrow-points like that in their heads today.

X

Coyote Meets Wind
and Some Others

X

COYOTE MEETS WIND AND
SOME OTHERS

 **C**OYOTE wanted to travel, to see some new country, so he took Mole and the children to the lodge of his friend, Badger. He asked Badger to care for them, and Badger said he would.

"I am going to hunt for enemies, *E-whe-whoot'-ken*, my friend," said Coyote. "I am going where there is great danger. Here is a little sack that belongs to me. Hang it on a tepee pole. If it should fall from the pole, you will know that I am dead. If it stays where you hang it, I am alive."

Badger hung the sack on a tepee pole, and Coyote started. He traveled for some time without meeting any enemies or getting into trouble. Then, one sun, he heard someone singing at the top of a high cliff. He went that way. He saw a sweat-house by the edge of the cliff. Inside was the singer. Hanging on a branch of a tree by the sweat-house was a suit of very fine buckskin clothes. Coyote liked that suit. He wanted it. He walked up to the sweat-house.

"I would like to sweat with you," he called, and the singer, who was *Sin-nee-iut*—Wind, stopped singing.

"I have used up all the water," he answered. "If you want to sweat-house you will have to get water down at the bottom of this cliff."

"I will get some water," Coyote said, and he picked up a water-basket and went down to the base of the cliff and filled it with water. He carried it back to Wind's sweat-lodge. "I have the water. I will pass it in to you," and he lifted the door-flap as if to hand the basket in to Wind. But, as Wind reached for the basket, Coyote threw all of the water on the hot stones in the sweat-house. That made such a steam that Wind was scalded to death.

Coyote laughed and put on the fine buckskin clothing, which was decorated with nice shell ornaments. Quite pleased with himself, Coyote walked away. Pretty soon he wished there was a gentle breeze to blow the shells and make them rattle. Right away his wish brought a soft breeze that tinkled the shells. Then Coyote wished for a stronger wind, and a strong wind came. It blew harder and harder, until it lifted Coyote off his feet and spun him through the air. His wishing had brought *Sin-nee-iut* back to life.

The wind carried Coyote to the top of the cliffs that watch over the Big Falls of the *Swah-*

netk'-qhu. There he grasped a little bush that grew out of the cliff. The bush was *Spet-zen'*—Hemp—and her sister. The Hemp sisters stripped Coyote of his stolen clothes, and they held him down under the edge of the cliff. Wind came along presently, looking for Coyote. "Where is *Sin-ka-lip'*?" he asked.

"He fell into the falls and was drowned," answered Hemp, and Wind believed her. He put on his clothes and went away. Then the sisters pulled Coyote up beside them. He was glad to be saved, and he said, "Now, what can I do to help you?"

"We barely exist," said Hemp. "All the time we suffer from thirst. We have to live on the little moisture that sprays up from the falls. It is not enough. We need water."

"I will give you water," said Coyote, and he walked off a few steps and threw water on the rocks around Hemp and her sister. Then, out of the cliff trickled some water. You will notice today that hemp grows only where the ground is wet.

Coyote left the Hemp sisters and walked until he came to a large encampment by a lake. Yelling that enemies were coming, he ran into the camp like he was being chased. The people were scared. They grabbed their weapons and made their canoes ready for war. Then Coyote talked to his *squas-tenk'*. He had it put all of the people to sleep. Coyote collected their weapons and food, which he loaded into one canoe. Then he broke all the other canoes and paddled out on the lake.

When the people awoke they hurried to make new weapons and new canoes. They knew who had tricked them. They started after Coyote. Seeing them coming, he caused a heavy fog with his medicine-power. The fog settled close to the water and all over the lake. None of the people could see into the fog—none but *Swa-lah'-kin*—Frog-woman. The fog did not bother her. She took the lead and guided the others. Not knowing that Frog-woman could follow through the fog, Coyote thought he was safe. He paddled his canoe to shore and went to sleep on the beach. There the people found and killed him.

Many moons later, *Sui-ah'*—Cougar—traveled through that country. He traveled high up along the mountain sides. As he came close to the death-place of Coyote, he became thirsty and went down to the lake. There he found what was left of Coyote. He collected the remains and stepped over Coyote three times, and Coyote returned to life.

"*Eh-ahe! Kes-sap tee-seh-eet!*" ("Eh! Long time sleep!") said Coyote, stretching and yawning.

"You have not been sleeping," corrected Cougar. "You were dead. You were killed by the Arrow Lakes people."

"May I go along with you, Big Teeth?" asked Coyote.

"Well, I prefer to travel alone," said Cougar, "but you may come with me, if you will promise to keep out of mischief."

Coyote said he would keep out of trouble, so they set out together. That night they camped on a mountain top. Cougar brought out a small bag of food. Coyote thought it would not be enough for the both of them. He was hungry— he was always hungry. Cougar read his thoughts.

"There is plenty here for the two of us," he said. "Eat all you want." So Coyote ate heartily. When he and Cougar had finished, he was surprised to see that the bag was as full of food as at first. Cougar told Coyote to throw the scraps away. Coyote did not want to do that. He thought that was wasteful. But Cougar insisted, and he threw away the scraps. Then they slept.

In the morning Cougar brought out another bag—a deer-bladder full of food—and, when they were through eating, the bladder was still full. That day, from the top of a mountain, Cougar pointed out his lodge.

"I must go home now to my children, as they are hungry," he said. "I will give you a bow and two arrows," and he gave them to Coyote. "This first arrow is to kill deer. Shoot it through a divide in a hill and you will kill a deer. This other arrow is for birds. Do not get them mixed. Do not shoot a bird with the deer-arrow and do not shoot a deer with the bird-arrow. If you use them wrong, you will lose the arrows."

After Cougar left him, Coyote tried his new arrows. He shot the deer-arrow through a divide and killed a deer. He ate the deer. Then he shot a pheasant with the bird-arrow, and he ate the pheasant. He saw another pheasant. He shot it with the deer-arrow, but it did not fall. It sat, with the arrow sticking through it. So he shot the bird-arrow, and the pheasant flew off with both arrows. It sailed down the mountain and out of sight. Coyote hated to lose those arrows, so he tried to follow the pheasant. He came to a tepee. He went in. By the fire sat *Char'-tups*— Fisher. The two lost arrows were there. Fisher had them.

"Long Tail," said Coyote, "I came to get those arrows."

"The arrows belonged to my older brother, *Sui-ah'*," answered Fisher. "I have found them and I will keep them. But I will give you two of my own arrows. They are like the others, and the rule is the same. Do not mix them when you shoot."

Coyote took Fisher's arrows and went away feeling good. But he soon forgot the rule for the arrows. He mixed them, shooting the wrong one first, and a pheasant flew off with both arrows. Following the pheasant, Coyote came to the lodge of *Pip-qus*—Marten, who had the lost arrows in his hand.

"No, I cannot give you these arrows," explained Marten. "They belonged to my older brother, Fisher. I found them, and I will keep them, but I will give you two of my own arrows. They are used the same way, by the same rule."

Marten gave Coyote two arrows, but it was not long before foolish Coyote forgot the rule and shot the wrong one and then the other, and both arrows were lost. He hunted for them until he grew tired. Then he decided to go home.

When he reached his tepee, he stopped outside to listen. He heard Badger crying. He crept close and peeked through the doorway, and his youngest son shouted:

"*Le-ee'-oo!*" ("Father!")

"Your father is dead," Badger said to the boy. "He never will come back."

"No!" the boy answered. "I see my father now! Look—at the doorway." He pointed. Then Badger saw Coyote peeking.

"You were dead," said Badger. "The little sack fell from the pole many moons ago."

"I was tired," Coyote replied. "I slept by the water. The Arrow Lakes people followed me. They found me sleeping. They killed me. Big Teeth found my bones and helped me back to life."

Coyote was glad to be home again, and Mole and the children were glad, too. So was Badger.

XI

Why Gartersnake Wears a Green Blanket

XI

WHY GARTERSNAKE WEARS A GREEN BLANKET

S UCK-Z'-CUM — Thunder-Bird —used to fly from the Warmland (South) once every snow to devour the most beautiful of the maidens. He always wanted a maiden as soon as he appeared —at his first rolling among the clouds. He would not stand for any delay. He came at the blooming of the woods-flowers, and then there was wailing in the villages—sorrow for the girl who must give herself to the monster. This maiden, chosen by the tribes because of her great beauty, would have to walk out and meet the monster, and be eaten. Then *Thing-that-hits* would not harm the other people. That was the custom. No one ever thought of trying to change it, of defying the terrible Thunder-bird.

It happened one spring that the girl who was loved by little *Sku-qua-wel'-hau*—Gartersnake —was chosen to be the sacrifice to Thunder-bird. That made Gartersnake very sad. He had no wish to live without her, so he decided to go with her when she went to meet the monster.

Thunder-bird could be seen high in the clouds when the maiden started toward the sacrifice-place. Putting on his best war-shirt, Gartersnake followed her. She looked around and saw him. She begged him to go back, to leave her. She did not want him to be killed, too. But Garter-snake hurried his steps and caught up with her.

"Oh, go back! Go back to our people," she said. "You cannot stand before the awful *Suck-z'-cum*. Let me die alone."

"No! If you must die, I will die with you," answered Gartersnake, and he kept by her side.

Soon they heard the noise of the monster's wings. The maiden cried, and Gartersnake felt weak, but he tried not to show his fear. Thunder-bird roared over them. His great wings shook the air and made the sky dark. He swooped low and from his mouth came a stream of fire. Gartersnake spat back.

"This person must be powerful," said Thunder-bird to himself. "He spits fire as I do." Then, thinking to discover his small enemy's weakness, Thunder-bird asked: "What do you fear? Of what are you afraid?"

"Nothing! There is nothing I fear," replied Gartersnake. "And you cannot hurt me. Nothing can hurt me. If you feel like fighting me, I will show you how to spit real fire. My fire-spit is worse than yours."

Thunder-bird believed those words, for none of the people ever had dared to talk to him like that. Only the frightened, wailing maidens ever had come to meet him. But he hoped to scare the other, and he spat a fearful streak of fire. Gartersnake then spat a stream of sizzling fire that flashed right in the monster's face. Thunder-bird couldn't stand that. He turned and fled, heading for the Warm-land. Spitting his hardest, Gartersnake ran after him, and not until he was sure that the monster really was beaten did Gartersnake stop chasing him. Then he shouted:

"A New People are coming to the world. From this day you will not come down out of the sky to eat people. You may roam the sky, but you shall make only rumblings and crashings in the storm."

Suck-z'-cum never returned to eat any more maidens or to destroy the tribes. But sometimes he clashes his wings and spits his fire through the clouds.

For his bravery the people gave Gartersnake a pretty green blanket with stripes on it. *Sku-qua-wel'-hau*, the Ground Twister, still wears that blanket.[1]

---

[1]*Sku-qua-wel'-hau.* Modified to *Chewelah*, this name has been applied to a small town and a creek in Stevens County, Washington. The townsite formerly abounded with garter-snakes.

XII

Coyote Quarrels With Mole

XII

COYOTE QUARRELS WITH MOLE

OYOTE and his wife, Mole, and their children were living by themselves, away from the winter encampment of the people. The other people did not want Coyote around, he was so lazy and tricky. Coyote and his family were poor that winter. They had only a little food, and that was supplied by the faithful Mole. Each day she would go out and gather herbs and moss and dried and shriveled *sko-qeeu* (rose-hips).[1] She did that to keep the five children from starving. And she carried all the wood and water, while Coyote loafed and practised his war songs.

One sun, as Mole was chopping a rotten stump for firewood, a little fawn jumped out of the stump. The deer family had put it there. The deer felt sorry for Mole. They wanted her to have the fawn for food.

Mole dropped her axe and caught the little deer. She told her oldest boy to run and tell his father to come with a knife and cut the fawn's throat.

---

[1]The fruit of the wild rose, *Rosa gymnocarpa*.

"Tell your father to hurry," said Mole, "because I cannot hold this fawn long. My strength will give out."

The boy ran fast to the tepee. He told Coyote what Mole had said.

"Go back to your mother and tell her to hold the fawn while I get my bow and arrows ready," Coyote ordered, and the boy ran back to his mother with the message.

Coyote ran out of the lodge and got a piece of dogwood, from which he made a bow. Then he ran to a service berry bush, where he cut two arrows. Then he ran back to his lodge to finish making his weapons. Taking feathers from his war bonnet, he feathered the arrows and, as he had no sinew for a bowstring, he tore the strings off his moccasins and made a string. Then he was ready to shoot the fawn.

All the while Mole was having a hard time holding the fawn. It struggled and kicked and fought to get away, and Mole's strength was leaving her. Her arms ached. She called to Coyote to hurry. He ran out of the lodge and tramped down the snow so he could kneel and shoot. He told Mole to let loose of the fawn so he could shoot it. Mole let go and Coyote shot his arrow, but the little deer fell just then and the arrow missed it. With his second and last arrow Coyote shot again as the fawn leaped up, and again Coyote missed. The fawn escaped into the woods.

Mole was disgusted and angry. She went back to the tepee. There she discovered that Coyote had eaten all the rose-hips, all the food that was left, while he was making his weapons. When Coyote came in, Mole spoke to him about that. They quarreled, and Coyote stabbed her with his flint knife. Mole ran out. Coyote followed. He meant to kill her. Mole changed herself into a real Mole as Coyote stabbed again. He stabbed the earth, and Mole quickly untied her little pouch of *tul-meen* (red facial paint) and put some of the paint on the point of the knife. Drawing the knife out of the ground, Coyote saw the red paint and thought it was blood. He was satisfied that his wife must be dead from that last blow.

Coyote soon found that he could not take care of his children without Mole's help. They could not live as they had before, so Coyote told the four oldest children to visit their "uncle," Kingfisher—Z-*reece'*, who was a good hunter and had plenty of food in his lodge. The four boys started for Kingfisher's home, and Coyote took his youngest and favorite son and went traveling. The youngest boy's name was *Top'-kan*.

They traveled many suns without getting much to eat. They were hungry when they came to a large prairie, where a woman dressed in red-painted buckskin was digging *spit-lum* (bitter-root). Seeing her digging reminded Coyote of his wife, and he wished that Mole were alive to dig roots for him to eat. He took *Top'-kan* off his back, where the little boy rode much of the time to keep from tiring, and told him to wait. Then Coyote went toward the strange woman.

"Tell me a story, tell me news, good woman," said Coyote upon getting near to the digger. But the woman did not take any notice of him. She kept on digging roots and cleaning them as she put them in her basket, which was strapped to her side.

Not so easily discouraged, Coyote walked closer, saying: "Tell me news. I am a traveler from a distant country."

"I will tell you a story," said the woman, and she turned angrily to Coyote. "Coyote deserted his children and killed his wife!"

Then Coyote recognized the woman as his own wife, Mole. She had followed him to watch over little *Top'-kan,* but Coyote had not known that. Grabbing his knife, Coyote ran at his wife. He meant to kill her, but she changed into a real mole and went underground and got away.

Coyote returned to *Top'-kan.* He picked the boy up, put him on his back, and resumed his journey. He sought new lands where his tricks and mischief-making were not known.

XIII

How Coyote Happened to Make the Black Moss Food

XIII

HOW COYOTE HAPPENED TO MAKE
THE BLACK MOSS FOOD

COYOTE and *Top'-kan* were traveling. Wherever the trail was rough, little *Top'-kan* rode on his father's back. They came to the lodge of *En-ze'-chen*— Wolf, an old man. He was busy skinning a beaver. After watching old Blood-Curdling Call for awhile, Coyote asked: *"En-ze'-chen*, how do you kill the *stun'-whu* (beaver)?"[1]

"It is at the beaver dam," answered Wolf. "I sit on the dam, with one leg in the water. As a beaver passes over my leg, I strike hard with a big stick. The *stun'-whu* cannot live after a blow like that."

"Ha-ha-eah!" Coyote laughed. "That is my way of killing the *stun'-whu!"*

Old Wolf said nothing. He knew that *Sin-ka-lip'*, the Imitator, had never killed beavers in that way. He suspected that Coyote soon would be in trouble.

---

[1]*Stun'-whu*—the old-time name for beaver. The modern name, applied since the advent of the fur traders, is *skal-weet-za,* which means "money fur."

Coyote took a heavy stick and went down to the beaver dam and sat with one leg in the water, as Wolf instructed. The beavers saw him. One of them said:

"Look! There is *Sin-ka-lip'!* He is trying to trick someone. Let us walk over his leg, and see what he does."

Two young beavers swam up to the dam. They climbed over Coyote's leg, and he struck hard with the heavy stick. He missed the beavers—they were too quick for him—but he hit his leg a terrific whack. He howled and danced with pain and rage, and then he tore into the beaver dam and threw the sticks and mud right and left. In a little while there was no dam there. He found the two beavers that had fooled him. They appeared to be dead.

"They will make good eating," he remarked, and he carried the beavers to where *Top'-kan* was playing. "You can wear these as ear ornaments while I am getting wood for a fire," Coyote told his son, and he tied the beavers to the little boy's ears, one to each ear.

As soon as Coyote was busy gathering wood, the beavers jumped up and ran, dragging *Top'-kan* behind them. They ran down the bank to the place where the dam had been. There they squirmed into different holes. That stretched

Top'-kan's ears in opposite directions. *Top'-kan* yelled, for the stretching hurt.

Hearing the cries of his son, Coyote ran to help him. He found poor *Top'-kan* braced between the holes and unable to move. There was nothing to do but to cut the thongs that held the beavers, which Coyote did. The beavers got away. Ever since that time the ears of coyotes have stood long and pointed.

No beaver to roast, Coyote and *Top'-kan* started traveling again. They went along until they came to a large lake. Resting in the water were many *si-mil'-ka-meen* (white swans). Coyote wanted one of those swans to eat, so he swam out into the lake. He kept under water, but the swans were not fooled. They knew he was there.

"Here comes *Sin-ka-lip'!*" they said. "See his tail floating! Let him catch a couple of us, and we will see what he will do."

So two of the younger swans allowed Coyote to catch them. He carried them to shore. They pretended to be dead. He tied them fast to *Top'-kan*. Then he climbed a pine tree to get the pitch-top, where *Kwil-kin*[2]—Porcupine— had gnawed. He wanted the pitch-top for fire-kindling.

Just as he got to the top of the tree, Coyote

---

[2]*Kwil-kin*—Pine-bough Head.

heard his son crying. He looked down and saw the swans flapping their wings. They were starting to fly. Coyote jumped, but his long hair braid caught on a branch of the pine tree and did not come loose. Coyote swung there, helpless. He could not untangle his hair.

The swans flew past the tree, past Coyote, and up into the sky. Dangling beneath them, tied to them by the thongs, was little *Top'-kan*. When the swans were high in the air they cut the thongs, and *Top'-kan* fell to the ground and was killed. Then Coyote took his flint knife and chopped off his hair braid, and dropped to the earth. He looked up at his hair hanging from the branch.

"You shall not be wasted, my valuable hair. After this you shall be gathered by the people. The old women will make you into food," he said.

That was Coyote's ruling near the Beginning. That is why his hair, the long black timber-hair, hangs from trees in the mountains. It is called *squil-lip*. It is the black moss that the people cook in pit-ovens.[3]

---

[3]This "black moss" is a pendulous lichen, a species of *Usnea*. It grows on trees and bushes in the mountains. From a short distance it looks very much like unkempt black or dark hair. Palatable and nutritious when cooked, it is considered a delicacy by the Indians.

The moss is cooked in pits that are eighteen inches to

Top'-kan did not stay dead. Coyote restored him to life by stepping over his body three times. Then they returned to their own country.

---

four feet deep and three to six feet in diameter, according to the quantity to be prepared. Rectangular pit-ovens sometimes are made, but they are uncommon.

Stones heated in a roaring fire are rolled into the pit, flooring it completely. They are covered with a thick carpet of clean green grass or leaves, and green twigs. Then there is a layer of camas roots, and on this is placed a compact heap of the black moss. This is covered with green grass or leaves. Tule-reed matting is spread over this, and the pit is mounded with about six inches of firmly packed soil. Nowadays, canvas or gunnysacking frequently takes the place of the reed matting.

At the beginning of the "filling-up" process, one or more thick sticks are planted in the pit. They are withdrawn after the dirt is piled on, leaving open shafts down to the bed of hot stones. Cold water is poured down the shafts, and the orifices are plugged to seal in the steam that is generated. A hot fire of logs is built on the pit-oven and maintained for about forty-eight hours. On the third or fourth day, after the ashes have cooled, the oven is opened and the food taken out.

The moss has melted and run together, forming a thick jelly-like substance bluish-black in color. It is cooled and then is sliced and eaten. Or, it may be dried and stored for future use, in which event it has to be heated or boiled before being served, and resembles molasses. Dried, it becomes hard and keeps indefinitely.

Many of the Indians today like to sweeten the freshly cooked moss with sugar.

The camas roots steamed with the moss are black when removed from the oven, and are deemed a delicious "side dish."

This method of cooking, called by the Okanogans *sil-kip-em* (cooking-in-the-ground), often is used for meats and for camas roots without the black moss ingredient. Some of the women cook apples with the black moss.

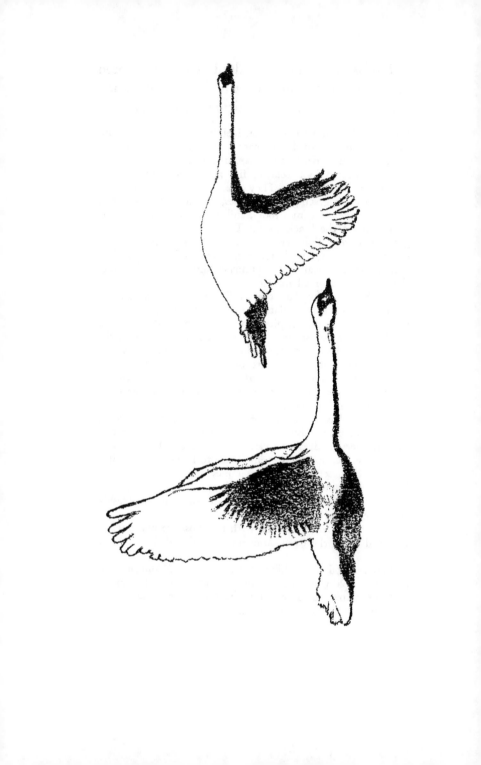

XIV

Why Spider Has Such
Long Legs

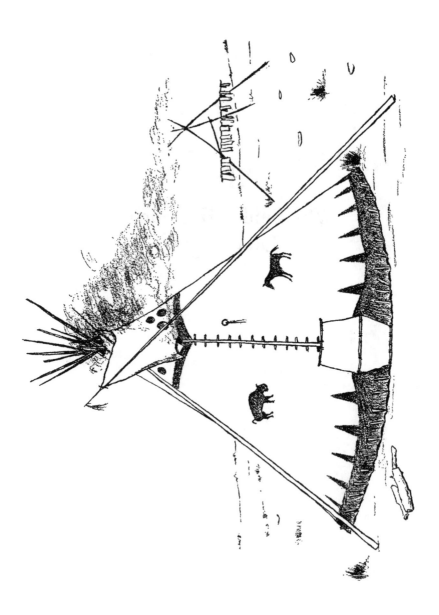

XIV

WHY SPIDER HAS SUCH LONG LEGS

TU-PEL—Spider, the Spinner—was a handsome warrior and good hunter. He lived with his grandmother, *Spu-wel'-kin*—Topknot, Woodpecker. Because he always brought home plenty of game, the maidens of the nearby villages all wanted to marry him. They would visit his lodge, hoping to win him.

Spider had a smoke-test for the maidens. When one came to see him, Spider would send his grandmother outside to close the smoke-flue. She would lap the ear-flaps so that the smoke could not get out. That would make the smoke thick in the lodge, and it would be hard to breathe in there.

Spider thought that he did not want a wife who could not stay in the smoke as long as he could, and he could stay in it a long time. Many maidens had tried the smoke-test and failed. But Spider always was nice to them. He would send them home with big packs of meat.

Stun'-whu — Beaver — had a very pretty daughter. She wanted to win Spider. She spoke to her father—asked his help. Beaver's medicine was strong. He gave his power to his daughter and told her how to use it. Then he sent her to Spider's lodge.

Spider liked the girl right away. He wanted her to be his wife. He did not care if she could not stand his smoke-test. Sending his grandmother out to close the smoke-flue, Spider pretended to make a smoky fire. But there was only a little smoke, and it was not the eye-stinging kind.

Beaver's daughter laughed. She sat on a spread robe and laughed at the smoke that Spider made, but she said nothing to Spider. With Beaver's medicine she called the blackest smoke, pitch smoke. It filled the lodge.

For most of that sun Beaver-girl and Spider sat in the lodge, on opposite sides of the fire. Spider's eyes finally became smoke-sick, and the pitch-smoke choked him. He spoke to Beaver-girl. She made no answer. Spider tried to think. That was hard, for the smoke blinded him, and his whole head ached. His own medicine could not help him. It was weak against the powerful *shoo'-mesh* of Beaver.

Spider wondered if the girl was still in the lodge. He spoke. No answer. He spoke again and again, many times, calling loudly through the smoke-darkness. Maybe the maiden was dead! Maybe the black smoke had killed her!

Spider felt his way around the fire. His foot struck the girl. She laughed. That made Spider ashamed. A woman was beating him in a trial of strength. He kicked Beaver-girl hard. He kicked her three times, and that made her very angry. She caught hold of one of Spider's legs, and she pulled and pulled, stretching the leg out, making it long. Then she pulled his other legs the same way. Spider could not stop her.

Well, when Woodpecker at last uncovered the smoke-flue and turned back the door-flap she saw a strange-looking grandson standing in the swirl of the outrushing smoke. He no longer was handsome. His body was small and his legs were very long and ugly.

Spu-wel'-kin was sorry for him. She knew that the maidens would not try to win him any more. So she ruled that Beaver-girl become his wife. Beaver's daughter was willing; she knew that *Tu-pel* always would provide plenty of game. And Spider was glad. He liked Beaver-girl even though she had treated him so roughly and spoiled his fine looks, and he forgave her for pulling him all out of shape—for making his legs so long.

XV
Why Badger Is So Humble

WHY BADGER IS SO HUMBLE

 ONE TIME *Why-ay'-looh*—Fox —and Coyote were living in the same lodge. The hunting was poor, and they became very hungry. They hunted hard every sun but did not find any game. At last Fox decided to leave that country and hunt somewhere else, but *Sin-ka-lip'* did not feel like going. So Fox left and Coyote stayed.

Coyote had nothing to eat but insects and leaves, although in a large camp not far away there was plenty of good food. Coyote knew it was useless to ask for food there, as those people hated him. But he intended to get some of that food. He began to scheme. The hungrier he grew the harder he schemed. Finally he had a plan.

Now, in that camp where the food was plentiful lived *E-whe-whoot'-ken*—Badger. He was a handsome person, was Sharp Claws, and he was a proud warrior and a good hunter. Much of the meat he killed he gave to poor persons. He was such a good hunter that many of the old people wanted him for a son-in-law. But Badger did not wish to marry any of the maidens in that village. He thought that sometime he would find a better wife in a far country.

One sun when Badger's four sisters went to the river to take their bath they came upon a pretty woman. She was sitting on the bank, painting her face with many colors. The sisters liked her appearance. They invited her to their lodge. They hoped that their proud brother would like her and make her his wife.

When Badger returned from hunting he was pleased to find the new woman in his lodge. He asked her to sit by his side, to sit in the place that was given to a wife. The woman smiled and said: "I am willing to be your wife, but first I must take some dried meat to my aged parents. Your sisters must go with me and help carry the meat."

Badger agreed to that, and the next sun the pretty woman and the sisters of Badger carried big packs of dried meat to the lodge that the woman said was the home of her aged parents. There the woman told them: "Wait outside while I take the meat in to my parents. They do not like to meet strangers."

The sisters waited outside while the meat was carried into the tepee, and they could hear talking, as if two or three persons were talking. Then, after all the meat was stored away in the lodge, the door-flap was thrown back and out stepped Coyote. He had been the pretty woman. He laughed over the joke he had played on Badger and the sisters.

The sisters were very angry, but they were unable to punish Coyote. They went home. They told Badger of the trick. He was angry and ashamed. It hurt his pride to be fooled in that way. He and his sisters did not want the people to find out, but somehow the people learned of what had happened.

A few suns later Badger wanted to take a sweat-bath. He went to the sweat-house. Some people were there. As he walked up, he heard someone say: "The proud, the handsome Badger is coming. He would not take a woman of his own tribe. He liked Coyote better! We do not want to sweat-house with him."

Those words shamed Badger. He turned from the sweat-house and went to look for Coyote. He found Coyote and chased him out of the country. Then he came home. He was proud no longer. He humbled himself before all the people and took from among them a wife. And he has been humble ever since, has *E-whe-whoot'-ken*.

XVI
Coyote Juggles His Eyes

XVI

COYOTE JUGGLES HIS EYES

A S HE WAS walking through the timber one morning, Coyote heard someone say: "I throw you up and you come down in!" Coyote thought that was strange talk. It made him curious. He wanted to learn who was saying that, and why. He followed the sound of the voice, and he came upon little *Zst-skaka'-na*—Chickadee—who was throwing his eyes into the air and catching them in his eye-sockets. When he saw Coyote peering at him from behind a tree, Chickadee ran. He was afraid of Coyote.

"That is my way, not yours," Coyote yelled after him.

Now, it wasn't Coyote's way at all, but Coyote thought he could juggle his eyes just as easily as Chickadee juggled his, so he tried. He took out his eyes and tossed them up and repeated the words used by the little boy: "I throw you up and you come down in!" His eyes plopped back where they belonged. That was fun. He juggled the eyes again and again.

Two ravens happened to fly that way. They

saw what Coyote was doing, and one of them said: "*Sin-ka-lip'* is mocking someone. Let us steal his eyes and take them to the Sun-dance. Perhaps then we can find out his medicine-power."

"Yes, we will do that," agreed the other raven. "We may learn something."

As Coyote tossed his eyes the next time, the ravens swooped, swift as arrows from a strong bow. One of them snatched one eye and the other raven caught the other eye.

"Quoh! Quoh! Quoh!" they laughed, and flew away to the Sun-dance camp.

Oh, but Coyote was mad! He was crazy with rage. When he could hear the ravens laughing no longer, he started in the direction they had gone. He hoped somehow to catch them and get back his eyes. He bumped into trees and bushes, fell into holes and gullies, and banged against boulders. He soon was bruised all over, but he kept on going, stumbling along. He became thirsty, and he kept asking the trees and bushes what kind they were, so that he could learn when he was getting close to water. The trees and bushes answered politely, giving their names. After awhile he found he was among the mountain bushes, and he knew he was near water. He came soon to a little stream and satisfied his thirst. Then he went on and presently he was in the pine timber. He heard someone laughing. It was *Kok'-qhi Ski'-kaka*—Bluebird. She was with her sister, *Kwas'-kay*—Bluejay.

"Look, sister," said Bluebird. "There is *Sin-ka-lip'* pretending to be blind. Isn't he funny?"

"Do not mind *Sin-ka-lip'*," advised Bluejay. "Do not pay any attention to him. He is full of mean tricks. He is bad."

Coyote purposely bumped into a tree and rolled over and over toward the voices. That made little Bluebird stop her laughing. She felt just a little bit afraid.

"Come, little girl," Coyote called. "Come and see the pretty star that I see!"

Bluebird naturally was very curious, and she wanted to see that pretty star, but she hung back, and her sister warned her again not to pay attention to Coyote. But Coyote used coaxing words; told her how bright the star looked.

"Where is the star?" asked Bluebird, hopping a few steps toward Coyote.

"I cannot show you while you are so far away," he replied. "See, where I am pointing my finger!"

Bluebird hopped close, and Coyote made one quick bound and caught her. He yanked out her eyes and threw them into the air, saying:

"I throw you up and you come down in!" and the eyes fell into his eye-sockets.

Coyote could see again, and his heart was glad. "When did you ever see a star in the sunlight?" he asked Bluebird, and then ran off through the timber.

Bluebird cried, and Bluejay scolded her for being so foolish as to trust Coyote. Bluejay took two of the berries she had just picked and put them into her sister's eye-sockets, and Bluebird could see as well as before. But, as the berries were small, her new eyes were small, too. That is why Bluebird has such berrylike eyes.

While his new eyes were better than none at all, Coyote was not satisfied. They were too little. They did not fit very well into his slant sockets. So he kept on hunting for the ravens and the Sun-dance camp. One day he came to a small tepee. He heard someone inside pounding rocks together. He went in and saw an old woman pounding meat and berries in a stone mortar. The old woman was *Su-see-wass*— Pheasant. Coyote asked her if she lived alone.

"No," she said, "I have two granddaughters. They are away at the Sun-dance. The people there are dancing with Coyote's eyes."

"Aren't you afraid to be here alone?" Coyote asked. "Isn't there anything that you fear?"

"I am afraid of nothing but the *stet'-chee-hunt* (stinging-bush)," she said.

Laughing to himself, Coyote went out to find a stinging-bush. In a swamp not far away he found several bushes of that kind. He broke off one of those nettle bushes and carried it back to the tepee. Seeing it, Pheasant cried: "Do not touch me with the *stet'-chee-hunt!* Do not touch me! It will kill me!"

But Coyote had no mercy in his heart, no pity. He whipped poor Pheasant with the sting-ing-bush until she died. Then, with his flint knife, he skinned her, and dressed himself in her skin. He looked almost exactly like the old woman. He hid her body and began to pound meat in the stone mortar. He was doing that when the granddaughters came home. They were laughing. They told how they had danced over Coyote's eyes. They did not recognize Coyote in their grandmother's skin, but Coyote knew them. One was little Bluebird and the other was Bluejay. Coyote smiled. "Take me with you to the Sun-dance, granddaughters," he said in his best old-woman's voice.

The sisters looked at each other in surprise, and Bluejay answered: "Why, you did not want to go with us when the morning was young."

"Grandmother, how strange you talk!" said Bluebird.

"That is because I burned my mouth with hot soup," said Coyote.

"And, Grandmother, how odd your eyes look!" Bluejay exclaimed. "One eye is longer than the other!"

"My grandchild, I hurt that eye with my cane," explained Coyote.

The sisters did not find anything else wrong with their grandmother, and the next morning the three of them started for the Sun-dance camp. The sisters had to carry their supposed grandmother. They took turns. They had gone part way when Coyote made himself an awkward burden and almost caused Bluejay to fall. That made Bluejay angry, and she threw Coyote to the ground. Bluebird then picked him up and carried him. As they reached the edge of the Sun-dance camp, Coyote again made himself an awkward burden, and Bluebird let him fall. Many of the people in the camp saw that happen. They thought the sisters were cruel, and the women scolded Bluebird and Bluejay for treating such an old person so badly.

Some of the people came over and lifted Coyote to his feet and helped him into the Sun-dance lodge. There the people were dancing over Coyote's eyes, and the medicine-men were passing the eyes to one another and holding the eyes up high for everyone to see. After a little Coyote asked to hold the eyes, and they were handed to him.

He ran out of the lodge, threw his eyes into the air, and said: "I throw you up and you come down in!"

His eyes returned to their places, and Coyote ran to the top of a hill.

There he looked back and shouted: "Where are the maidens who had Coyote for a grandmother?"

Bluejay and Bluebird were full of shame. They went home, carrying Pheasant's skin, which Coyote had thrown aside. They searched and found their grandmother's body and put it back in the skin, and Pheasant's life was restored. She told them how Coyote had killed her with the stinging-bush.

XVII
Why Marten's Face Is Wrinkled

XVII

WHY MARTEN'S FACE IS WRINKLED

THE FACE of *Pip-qus*—Marten —has not always been wrinkled and homely. Long ago it was smooth and handsome. That was before Marten disobeyed his older brother, *Char'-tups*, Long Tail—Fisher. Before that time, too, Marten would eat only birds and squirrels. Fisher liked venison and fat.

In their country was a mountain that Fisher told Marten not to go near. Fisher told him never to go there, but he gave no reason. Marten could not understand why he should not go to that place; he often noticed his brother setting out in that direction. He did not know that Fisher went to visit a pretty young woman.

For a long time Marten obeyed his brother. Then, one sun, he forgot his brother's words. He was trying to catch some birds. They flitted on ahead of him, going toward the mountain. After awhile he came to the foot of the mountain. He saw a bluejay sitting in a tree. He shot the bluejay with an arrow, and the bluejay fell down through the smoke-hole of a lodge.

Marten walked into the lodge to get the bird. Beside the fire was a pretty young woman. She prepared food for her visitor. She gave him dried venison and berries mixed with fat. Marten never ate that kind of food. The sight and the smell of the dried venison and the fatty berries made him feel sick. He pushed the food away. That insulted the young woman. The food was the best she had.

"You shot my comb, my bluejay," she said, "and now you refuse to eat my food."

She grabbed Marten by the hair and pitched him into the fire, and rubbed his smooth handsome face in the hot ashes until he yelled with pain. Then she threw him out of the lodge.

Marten's face was burned all over. He was almost killed. For some time he lay on the ground. When some of his strength came back, he got up and sneaked home. He did not want to be seen, he was so full of shame. He hid between the coverings of the lodge,[1] and there he was when his brother returned from hunting.

As he was accustomed to do, Fisher called Marten to catch his load of fresh meat. Marten

---

[1] The lodge coverings here referred to were layers of lapped tule mats. They were quite effective in keeping out the weather. Tanned deer skins also were used for tepee coverings in primitive times, but rarely were buffalo hides available, as among the tribes nearer to and in the buffalo country.

did not answer. Long Tail called again. Then Marten mocked his brother, which made Fisher angry. He found Marten and pulled him from his hiding place. Fisher intended to punish him, but he changed his mind upon seeing how terribly Marten's face was burned, and he took some grease and rubbed it on the burns.

After a few suns Marten grew very hungry. He would not eat the meat that his brother brought home, and he was not able to hunt for his kind of food. In a few more suns he was so weak and thin that he had to eat something or die. He licked a few drops of grease from his face. It was the venison grease that Fisher had put on the burns. Marten was surprised. The grease tasted good. After that he ate venison and liked it. He still likes such food.

Marten's face finally healed, but the deep burns left many wrinkles, and that is why he is called *Pip-qus*—Wrinkled Face.

The young woman who was the cause of those changes became Fisher's wife.

XVIII
Crawfish and Grizzly Bear

XVIII

CRAWFISH AND GRIZZLY BEAR

KEE-LAU-NAW—Grizzly Bear —lived in a big forest. He would not let anybody hunt there. People who went there to hunt never came back. Grizzly Bear ate them.

Because they could not get any of the game in Grizzly Bear's forest, the people began to starve. They danced and prayed, asking their powers to help them. One sun the prayers of *Jī'-hah*—Crawfish—were answered. He received strong medicine. Then he started for Grizzly Bear's forest.

Owl, who was Grizzly Bear's lookout, saw Crawfish coming. Owl hooted to warn Grizzly Bear, who rushed out of his lodge, roaring his war cry. Crawfish pretended not to see him, and that hurt Grizzly Bear's pride, and he roared louder and gnashed his teeth. But Crawfish paid no attention.

Grizzly Bear rushed back into his lodge and changed his summer teeth for his new, sharp winter teeth. Out he came again. He thought that Crawfish surely would be scared now, for the winter teeth made him look very fierce. But Crawfish still paid no attention. Grizzly Bear went back to his lodge and put on his sharpest claws, and he hurried out, waving his big arms and showing the sharp claws.[1] But Crawfish acted as if he didn't know such a person as Grizzly Bear was around. Crawfish just kept walking along.

Grizzly Bear was used to being treated with respect. He could not understand why Crawfish was not afraid, and he was boiling with rage. He decided to finish Crawfish without more delay. He charged. One quick, strong hug, and there would be no more Crawfish—so thought Grizzly Bear. But just as he expected to grab Crawfish, that person lifted his two red fingers and pinched Grizzly Bear, pinched him hard.

Holding his enemy tight, Crawfish drew him close, pulled him right up to his sharp red nose. Grizzly Bear was badly scared. He believed he was about to be eaten. He was so frightened that he spit froth and foam into the face of Crawfish. That disgusted Crawfish, but he did not let go. He pinched all the harder, and Grizzly Bear cried in pain and begged for mercy.

"*Kee-lau-naw*," said Crawfish, "you will have

---

[1] The grizzly bear was supposed to go into winter quarters with teeth and claws dulled from usage, and to emerge in the spring with them renewed in sharpness.

to leave these woods. You will have to go away and leave these woods for the hunters. You must go high in the mountains and make your home. There, away from the people, you can harm them no longer, and you are not to bother people unless they attack you. Start now for the highest mountains. Do not come back! Go! Hurry away from here!"

Grizzly Bear agreed to go. He ran until he found himself in some low mountains. There he stopped and looked around. He could see nobody following him, and he said to himself: "*Jĭ'-hah*, you think you can make me live in the high mountains. I shall not go. I am going home." And he turned and headed for his forest. He was in a hurry to get back. He ran. He started to run between two big red trees. That is, he thought they were trees. But they were the fingers of Crawfish, and they closed around him. They lifted him up and carried him to the place he had reached when he decided to return home.

Grizzly Bear spit in the face of Crawfish again, but that only caused Crawfish to pinch the harder. Then Grizzly Bear begged to be free. He promised to do as Crawfish told him, so Crawfish let him go.

Up hill and down, and up again, ran Grizzly Bear, until he had traveled a long way. He stopped to rest, leaning against a tree, and he looked back over his trail. He saw no one coming, and he changed his mind about going further into the mountains. His temper was sour and he whispered to himself: "*Jī'-hah* cannot make me do that. He cannot keep me from my old home. I am going back where I always have lived."

He had barely finished those words when he felt the supposed tree against which he was leaning lift him off the ground. Two big red fingers tightened about his middle. The fingers of Crawfish held him fast. Surprised and badly frightened, Grizzly Bear thought his enemy would show no mercy now. He kicked and groaned, and then he pretended to be half-dead from the squeezing, but Crawfish would not let go.

Then Grizzly Bear cried: "Do not kill me! I will never return to the forest. I will go to the highest mountains, and stay there." This he said five times, and Crawfish let him go.

Crawfish warned: "If you do come back, I will catch you and kill you. This is your last chance. Do not ever come back to the lower country. From this sun your lodge must be in the highest mountains, up where the mists are thickest, where the snows are deepest. A New People are coming to the world. You shall not starve them by keeping all the game to yourself. Go and do not look back!"

Grizzly Bear was glad to get away. He ran, and he did not look back. He did not stop running until he was in the highest range of mountains. There he has made his home ever since.

Crawfish returned to his own country. The people there were glad. Now they could hunt and get plenty of food and plenty of skins.

Since the time that Crawfish whipped Grizzly Bear there have been fewer times of famine.

XIX

Coyote and Wood-Tick

XIX

COYOTE AND WOOD-TICK

TIRED and hungry, Coyote sat in his hunting-camp tepee. Game was scarce, and he had not found any deer for a long time. "I wish I had some deer meat," he said, and he heard something fall at the doorway of the tepee. He got up and looked. *Eh-ahe!* On the ground was a pack of venison! That made Coyote feel good. He quickly kindled a fire and cooked a big meal. He filled his belly and had a good sleep. Next morning he was up and out hunting before Sun's light reached into the woods.

"I will find a deer today," thought Coyote. "That pack of meat at my doorway last night shows that there are deer in this country."

But he did not see a deer all day. By night he was very hungry again and very tired. Resting on his robes in the tepee, he wished aloud for more venison, and another pack of it came bouncing through the doorway. Coyote looked out to see who had brought the meat, but there was no one in sight.

"Now, who answers my wishes so promptly?"

he asked himself. "I must find out tomorrow night."

He hunted all the next day without success, and that night, instead of lying on his robe to rest, he crouched just inside the door-flap. Then he wished for deer meat. *Eh-ahe!* There it was —right at his feet—a pack of venison that would last him half-a-moon. Jumping through the doorway, he saw a woman disappearing in the woods. At last he knew—his neighbor. He could not mistake her. He recognized her flat shiny head. She was *Kuk-chil'-ken*—Wood-tick. She had no husband.

In his mean, ungrateful way, Coyote yelled: "You shiny-head! You flat-headed woman! I thought a maiden worth having was favoring me."

Wood-tick no longer was a young woman, and that insult made her very angry. She was used to being treated with respect, for she was the ruler of all the deer. She did not answer Coyote; she did not even look around. She went on as if she had not heard him.

Coyote returned to his camp and ate some of the venison she had given him. That bundle of venison lasted many suns, but it could not last forever. When the last scrap was gone, Coyote wished for more, but no pack of venison fell at his doorway. He wished many times and in a very loud voice. No meat came. Then he realized that *Kuk-chil'-ken* must still be very angry.

"I will make up with her," Coyote remarked, and he walked over to her lodge. Wood-tick would not look at him when he entered. She turned her back and would not answer his greeting. Coyote saw that he could not make up with her, so he grabbed her by the neck and threw her to the ground. He pounded her head with a rock, making her head even flatter than before.

"That's what you get for being stubborn," said Coyote, and he tossed Wood-tick's body to one side.

Wood-tick's tepee was full of meat, so Coyote stayed there and ate all he could hold. In the morning he put on Wood-tick's robes and went outside to call the deer, as she had done every morning.

He used her words: *"Kat-ch-lhn, s'scooly-whn!"*[1] ("Run, deer!")

The deer came. They ran out of the woods, one after the other, in a long line. They ran straight to the lodge. Coyote held up a part of the lodge-covering, as Wood-tick always had done, and the deer went right on through the tepee. Following Wood-tick's custom, Coyote

---

[1]*S'scooly-whn*—This is supposed to be in Wood-tick's dialect. *Kat-ch-lhn* is Okanogan for "run."

shot the last deer in the line—the largest buck. That was the rule.

Each morning after that Coyote called the deer and shot the largest buck. He did that for a long time, and he had plenty to eat. But after awhile he grew tired of buck meat and wanted a young deer for a change. So he shot a fawn. That scared the other deer; they knew something was wrong.

"That person is not our mistress!" they said. "The eyes are not hers. They are too slant. That must be *Sin-ka-lip'*!"

The deer scattered and vanished in the woods. At the same time all the dried venison that was stored in the lodge came to life and followed the main herd. On their way out of the tepee, the venison-deer picked up Wood-tick's body and carried it on their backs, and Wood-tick came to life, too. Coyote's fine buckskin clothes peeled off him and went along after the venison-deer, and the whole herd kept on going until it reached the mountains, where the deer have remained ever since.

As soon as Coyote could collect his senses, he hurried to save what scraps of meat there might be left. He found a little. This he gathered and hid. Some he put behind logs, some in brushy places and some in the ground. But, a little later, when he went to the hiding-places, he had another surprise. Behind the logs, where he had hidden meat and bones, there was nothing but dried bark and dead tree limbs, and in the ground caches he found only stones! Naked and hungry, Coyote went home. Mole, his wife, made new clothes for him.

Old Maid Wood-tick rules the deer to this day. That is why there are wood-ticks on the backs of all the deer.

XX
Why Mosquitoes Bite People

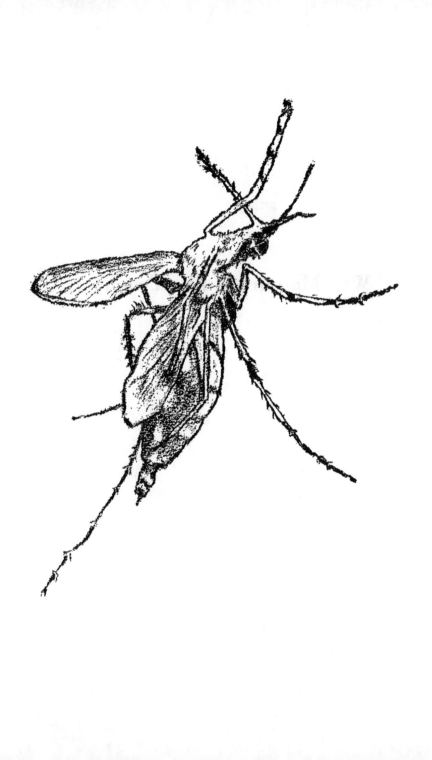

XX
WHY MOSQUITOES BITE PEOPLE

 THERE were five brothers. The smallest was *Se-lux*—Mosquito. He was lazy and greedy—greedy for blood. When his brothers killed game, they always gave him blood for his share. He never cooked it. He liked it uncooked.

Each night the brothers made Mosquito go to their sweat-house to seek *shoo'-mesh*, as he was the only one of the five who had not received medicine-power. One night he heard voices whispering as he walked toward the sweat-house, and he was afraid. He ran and told his brothers. They called him a coward and whipped him. Then they made him go to the sweat-house to spend the night. Mosquito crawled in there and cried himself to sleep.

Late in the night Mosquito was awakened by shouts and cries, the cries of his brothers. Enemies were killing them in their lodge. Soon the enemy people came to the sweat-house to kill little Mosquito. They jabbed their spears into the sweat-house. Mosquito daubed red paint on the spear-points. Believing the red paint was the blood of the boy, the enemies went away.

Next morning, after Sun trailed high, Mosquito sneaked out of the sweat-lodge and went to his brothers' tepee. There he found them. They were dead.

Mosquito felt very sad. He cried and cried. After awhile he walked down to the river and made a canoe. Then he floated in it down the river, and he cried all the time. He sang his song for the dead. He stuttered when he talked or sang; he could not help it. The song he sang was:

"*O-O-O! La-la! Co-pah-pool-ee-la kecht-kah!*" ("O-O-Oh! La-la! The-They kil-killed m-my brothers!")

He floated a long way down the river. He came to a big camp. The people saw him, and they shouted: "Come ashore and eat choke-cherries," but Mosquito did not stop. He floated on in his canoe and sang his mournful song.

He came to a second encampment. The people there shouted: "Come here, come here, *Se-lux!* Come and eat *ollalees* (berries)."

"O-Oh! N-No!" Mosquito answered, in his stuttering voice, and he floated on down the river. He came to a third encampment. Many people were there.

"There comes *Se-lux*," they said. "He likes blood."

Some of the people called to him to come and eat. Mosquito refused, and he was floating on by when they told him they could give him some uncooked blood. At that, he turned his canoe and paddled to shore. He tied the canoe fast, so it could not drift away, and went to the feast. While he was eating, filling himself with blood in his greedy way, some of the people shoved his canoe out on the river. The current carried it away. Then they told him that the canoe was gone.

Mosquito did not want to lose the canoe. He ran. He could not run fast—his stomach was too full. In his haste, he tripped and fell on a stick, which pierced his stomach and let out all the blood. From the wound flew a little fly. It alighted on a cottonwood tree.

"O-Oh! The-They kil-killed m-my brothers!" it sang.

The people heard the song. They spoke to the little fly: "When the future generations come, you will sing your song for the dead, and you will live on the blood of men—on the blood of people," they said. "That shall be your revenge for the death of your brothers."

XXI

The Gods of the Sun
and the Moon

XXI

THE GODS OF THE SUN AND THE MOON

MOLE WAS lonely. Coyote was away on one of his long trips. Mole would not have felt so lonesome if all her children had been with her. But there were only two left with her at home. The others had grown up and gone separate ways, as families do. The two that were left were boys. They were little.

Every sun Mole became more lonely. One day she saw a rock of odd shape. She liked it. She pretended it was Coyote; she made love to it. After it she named the older of her two small boys. She named him *Stee-qu'-lot*—Heated-Rock-Child. The rock was warmed by the sun. On another day, while digging roots she found a root that was white. It pleased her. As her smallest son's skin was light in color, she named him after the root. She named him *Swee'-elt*—White Root.

The moons passed and Coyote did not return. The boys grew. *Swee'-elt* told his mother that he could hear whispers coming up from the ground, and he asked her the reason.

"You are named after the roots," Mole explained. "The roots are your relatives. They call to you."

Stee-qu'-lot said that he could hear the rocks whispering to him, whispering sounds of friendship, and his mother told him that the rocks were his relatives.

Coyote finally came home. He found his sons grown to fine big boys, and he was glad. He was sorry that he had stayed away so long. He took the boys to himself to train. Every morning he got them up and made them swim in the cold river; he taught them to pray for strong medicine-powers. He was preparing them to meet hardships, to become good warriors. They became strong in body and spirit, and Mole was proud of them. *Swee'-elt* was handsome and white of skin, while *Stee-qu'-lot* was red of skin and strong and long of limb. He was a good hunter.

Coyote heard there was to be a big council in another country to decide on who should be the gods of *Kya'-len-whu*—the Sun—and *Skuk'-ach Kya'-len-whu*, the Night Sun—Moon. Coyote told his sons about the council. They wanted to go. They killed game, enough to last their parents while they were at the council. As they were leaving, Coyote suddenly decided to go with them. That left poor Mole all alone.

When Coyote and his sons reached the council they found the people worried. The people said they had not found anyone suited to take charge of either Sun or Moon. Many of the people had sought those honors, traveling in the Sun-lodge or the Moon-lodge across the sky, but all had failed. They either were too hot or too cold or too bright or too dim.

"I will be the Sun-god," declared Coyote, and the people allowed him to try. He took the Sun-lodge across the sky. But he watched everything that the people did. Seeing people in secret love, he yelled down to them, much to their embarrassment. He told on those who were hiding. The people were glad when that day was over. They lost no time in taking Coyote from the Sun-lodge. Then they asked Coyote's sons to try, but the sons refused. They wanted to remain on the earth.

Now, among those at the council was *Swa-lah'-kin*—Frog-woman. She was old and ugly, but she was in love with *Swee'-elt,* the white-skinned. Her special medicine was the rain. She caused a big rain to fall, and everything got sopping wet; the people were soaked to the skin and could not get dry, as all their fires were put out. All the fires but Frog-woman's were killed. Everybody shivered with cold—everybody but Frog-woman.

Swee'-elt did not know that Frog-woman's heart was soft toward him. He suggested to his brother that they go to her lodge and get dry by her bright fire. *Stee-qu'-lot* did not want to go. Knowing that Frog-woman loved his brother, he warned *Swee'-elt;* he told him to keep away—told him she was bad and powerful. But *Swee'-elt* became so cold that he went to her lodge by himself. Frog-woman was dressing a deer skin by the fire. Her lodge was warm and dry. *Swee'-elt* was glad he had come.

Looking up at him, Frog-woman said: "My husband! Take your place on the honored robe of your lodge."

Startled, *Swee'-elt* did not cross to the robe. Instead, he sat down near the entrance. He knew he should leave, but he did want to get warm. Frog-woman coaxed him to move to the husband-robe, but he shook his head and stayed by the doorway. Seeing that her coaxing was of no use, Frog-woman became angry. Suddenly, she changed herself into a real frog and jumped—smack!—at the young man's smooth white face. She struck his cheek and clung there. "Now," said Frog-woman, "you cannot leave me. Not if you go to the edge of the world will you ever get another wife!"

Swee'-elt tried to take Frog-woman off his cheek. He tugged and scraped in vain. All the people came and tried to take her off. Nothing could budge Frog-woman. The people even tried to cut her off and to burn her loose from his cheek, but she did not move. At last *Swee'-elt* gave up hope. Ashamed of his appearance, he decided what to do. He said to the people: "I will take charge of the Moon-lodge. I will go with it across the sky."

Stee-qu'-lot wished to be near his unhappy brother, so he said: "I will take charge of the Sun-lodge. I will take it across the sky."

In his Moon-lodge, *Swee'-elt* travels by night. That is because he is ashamed of his ugly wife. He hates her. She still clings to his cheek. Sometimes you can see her when the nights are clear. And if a frog is killed and laid on its back or held belly toward the sky, you will see a cloud-blanket spread over the Sun or the Moon. The brother-gods always hide their faces from frogs placed in that way. Perhaps they think that the frogs are trying to make love to them.

Because he is of the heated-rock, *Stee-qu'-lot* is well suited to sit in the Sun-lodge. *Swee'-elt*, being related to the white roots in the cool ground, is suited to stay in the Moon-lodge. His white face gives the Moon its light. That dark spot on his face is the hated Frog-woman. Moon-light is cool, because *Swee'-elt* was of the root-growing earth. His descendants are the white-skinned people. The descendants of *Stee-qu'-lot* are the red-skinned people.

When *Swee'-elt* left the council-camp to sit in the Moon-lodge he said: "In the future handsome warriors will marry homely women, and pretty women sometimes will marry homely men."

What *Swee'-elt* said is true to this day. He made it so from the Beginning.

XXII

Porcupine Learns the
Sun Dance

PORCUPINE LEARNS THE SUN-DANCE

THE *Khaka'-malh*—Fly-people— had the *Swen-qhum* (Sun-dance) first. The Sun-dance was theirs. It was their medicine. Many people wanted to learn the Sun-dance, to discover the power of the Flies, and many went to the Flies' village to learn the dance. But none ever returned. They were eaten by the crawlers that hatched from the eggs of the Flies. The *Khaka'-malh* kept their secret well.

One time Coyote went to the dance. As he danced, he became covered with eggs. Crawlers hatched from the eggs and ate him—ate most of him. What was left the Flies threw outside their camp. There the remains were found by Fox, who stepped over them three times. That restored Coyote to life.

Then Coyote went in search of someone to help him learn the secret of the Sun-dance. He met *Kwil-kin*—Porcupine, a brave man. He asked Porcupine to go back with him to the Fly village, and Pine-bough Head went. When they got to the camp, Coyote told Porcupine to go and dance while he watched. So Porcupine went on in and danced with the Flies. They laid eggs all over him. But the eggs did not bother Porcupine. Every little while he would shake himself hard, and the creepers that had crawled from the eggs would be killed on his sharp quills.

The Flies laid more and more eggs on Porcupine, and he kept on shaking himself and killing the crawlers; he was too much for the Flies. He killed all of them, too, except a very few small ones. These he permitted to live.

"Hereafter, Flies will not kill anybody," Porcupine told the little Flies. "There shall be no more big Flies to kill people. After this, only that which is dead shall be the egg-laying place of the Flies."

That was how the Flies lost the secret of their Sun-dance and their medicine-power. Because of Porcupine it no longer was a secret. The New People, when they came, were able to learn the Sun-dance.

XXIII

En-am-tues—The Wishing Stone

XXIII

EN-AM-TUES—THE WISHING STONE

THERE were three brothers, all great warriors. They lived in the Okanogan country. *Choo'-pahk*—Sticking—was the oldest; the second brother was *Scra'-kan*—Copper—and the youngest was *Nak-ka'-tuya*—Cut-up.

Among the Kalispel people lived a maiden named *Scoo'-malt*—Virgin. Her father was chief of the Kalispels.

One sun *Scoo'-malt* filled a basket with camas roots and started for the Okanogan country. She hoped to please the handsome, coppery *Scra'-kan* and become his wife. Upon reaching the summit of the range overlooking the Okanogan Valley from the east, she stopped to make herself beautiful. She combed and braided her long black hair and painted her face with red earth paint.

In their dreams the three brothers saw *Scoo'-malt* coming, and they went to meet her. Each asked her to marry him, and then the younger brothers fought. *Nak-ka'-tuya* slashed the shoulders off *Scra'-kan*, while *Scra'-kan* knocked

Nak-ka'-tuya down and kicked him into a long heap, flat on the ground.

Coyote came along as the brothers were fighting, and he laughed at seeing them fighting so hard over the Kalispel maiden. He thought it was a good joke, but his glee angered the girl, and she spoke sharply to him. Her words, in turn, angered Coyote. He would show the maiden that she could not talk that way to him. With the help of his great medicine-power he moved the brothers back to where they had been when they started to meet *Scoo'-malt,* and he changed them into mountains. Then he made *Scoo'-malt* helpless by turning her lower body into stone.

Taking her basketful of *et-quah* (camas), *Scoo'-malt* threw it back to her people, to the Kalispel country, so that none would grow in the land of the Okanogans, and she transformed the rest of herself into stone, to remain there in sight of her stone lovers forever.

Coyote was amused. To the stone maiden, he said: "Because you are a stranger in this place, you will help the coming generations by giving them good luck, but they will have to pay you to make their wishes happen." Then he turned to the mountains that had been warriors, and said: "*Choo'-pahk,* because you are proud and would not take part in the fight, you will stand with your head high and stately. You, *Scra'-kan*, because a virgin of another land came to court you, will be loved always by the women for your handsome coppery body. The women will like pieces of it for decorating their arms and hands. *Nak-ka'-tuya*, because you were beaten and kicked to the ground, you will lie in shame as a mountain ridge for other generations to see."

That is why *Choo'-pahk* (Mt. Chopaka) looks so proud and fine. *Scra'-kan*, nearby, to the north and west, stands without shoulders, a sharp-pointed peak (in British Columbia). Across the valley of the *Similkameen* River lies *Nak-ka'-tuya* (Mt. Richter, B. C.)

The maiden still sits on the summit where she stopped that day long ago to comb her hair and paint her face with the red earth paint. The people call her *En-am-tues*—Sitting-on-the-summit. The place where she sits is *Mock-tsin*—Knoll-between-a-divide. There the people have gone for many generations to ask for good luck and to pay for their asking with gifts so that their wishes would come true.[1]

---

[1]*En-am-tues* is known to the whites as the *Tee-hee-hee* stone. *Tee-hee-hee*, which is not an Okanogan word, may be a comparatively modern corruption of the verb meaning "to wish" in the Chinook jargon, the old-time trade language of the Northwest. Derived from the pure Chinook *tikekh*, "to wish" in the jargon is given variously as: *t'keh, te-ke, tik-eh, tik-eigh, tak-eigh, tick-ey, tikky,* and so forth.

The "wishing stone," or Camas-woman, as it frequently is called, is one of many wishing stations or shrines in the Northwest where the Indians made offerings. To pass Camas-woman without depositing a gift was said to bring sorrow and ill-luck. In return for even the smallest gift, the older generations of Indians believed she would grant any wish that might be asked. The sick supplicated for health, the poor for worldly goods, the ambitious for success in war, the chase, love, and other undertakings.

After the Indians' contact with the fur-traders, coin entered largely into the gifts, and the white men, learning of the Camas-woman's influence, robbed her of all her wealth.

When the Colville Reservation was thrown open to settlement in 1900, a prospector dynamited the shrine to see if it concealed anything of value.

The stone, originally about five feet in height, is now a pile of its shattered parts. After it was blasted, some of the Indians gathered up the fragments and heaped them to a height of six or seven feet. Mourning Dove remembers when the stone was intact.

En-am-tues, situated on a divide overlooking the Okanogan Valley from the east, is seven miles west and south of Molson, Washington. One of the main cross-country trails passed by it, but there are no modern roads in the vicinity.

The camas which the maiden threw back to her people is the "black camas" that grows on Camas Prairie near Calispell Lake, Pend Oreille County, Washington. Kalispel Indians who dig the root receive as high as a dollar a gallon for it from people of their own and other tribes. The Kalispel country always has been noted for its rich camas grounds.

The name, *Scra'-kan,* applied to one of the brother-mountains, is a modern Okanogan word that originally was used to designate the copper kettles traded to the Indians by the fur companies. Before the coming of the whites, gold nuggets and copper were made into bracelets, the pieces strung together. An ornament of this kind was called *skel-ear-qu-nekst',* which means "circle-around-the-wrist," and this word was the only one by which either of the metals was known.

XXIV

Chickadee Makes a
Shoó-Mesh Bow

CHICKADEE MAKES A *SHOO'-MESH* BOW

CHICKADEE wanted to cross the river where Elk had his trail. Elk crossed the river at the same place each sun. Chickadee waited for him there. When Elk came, Chickadee said: "*Ste-eel'-tza,* my grandfather. Take me across on your back."

Now, Elk was not Chickadee's grandfather, but Chickadee wanted to please Elk and gain his favor. Elk agreed to carry the little boy across the river. He took Chickadee on his back and waded into the water. With his flint knife, Chickadee began to cut the back of Elk's neck.

"*Zst-skaka'-na,* what are you doing?" asked Elk.

And Chickadee answered: "Grandfather, I am only scratching your neck."

Elk went on. Soon he thought that Chickadee was scratching too hard, and again he asked what the boy was doing.

"Grandfather, I am only scratching your neck," said Chickadee, but all the time he was cutting, cutting with his flint knife. Just as Elk reached the shore, Chickadee made a last cut and Elk fell dead with a broken neck. Chickadee was glad. He wanted one of Elk's ribs for a bow. Such a bow would have strong *shoo'-mesh*. He skinned Elk with his knife. As he finished taking off the hide, Mother Wolf walked up. She had hidden her two children close by in their cradle that was hung on a tree. Mother Wolf looked greedily at the elk meat.

"Go and get your little cousins," she said. "I left them on a tree by the trail."

Chickadee knew that she wanted to steal the meat, but he did not let on that he knew. He ran along the trail and found the children, but he did not take them to their mother. He carried them in the opposite direction, running far with them. Then he hurried back to Mother Wolf.

"I could not find your babies," he said.

"Why, they are on a tree close by the trail," said Mother Wolf, who thought that Chickadee could not find them. "Look again for them," and Chickadee ran to where he had left the children and carried them still farther away. He hurried back to Mother Wolf.

"No, I cannot find your babies," he said.

Mother Wolf sent him once more. As soon as he was gone she started cutting the elk meat into small pieces. By the time Chickadee returned, the meat was all cut up. Chickadee did not have the children, of course, so Mother Wolf finally had to go for them.

"Do not eat any of the meat until I come back," she told Chickadee. "Wait, and we will eat together," and she started down the trail. It took her a long time to find her children.

Chickadee began to carry the meat away as soon as Mother Wolf was out of sight. He took it to a high cliff, to a ledge halfway up the wall of the cliff. He made several trips, and he finished carrying all the meat there just before Mother Wolf returned with her children. She followed Chickadee's tracks to the foot of the cliff, and then she looked up and saw him sitting on the ledge and roasting the meat over a fire.

"*Zst-skaka'-na,* throw down a mouthful of meat for your little cousins," said Mother Wolf.

"Open their mouths. I will throw down a mouthful to each," answered Chickadee.

Mother Wolf opened the mouths of the little wolves, and into their mouths Chickadee dropped two hot stones that he had wrapped in fat. They swallowed the hot stones and were killed. Mother Wolf was not watching them. She was looking up at Chickadee, hoping he would throw her some meat.

"Now open your mouth, Mother Wolf," he instructed, and when her jaws were wide open Chickadee dropped a big rock, red hot and wrapped in fat. It slid down Mother Wolf's throat, and she fell over, dead.

Chickadee now dried the remainder of his meat in peace, and from one of Elk's ribs he made a bow. It had strong power.

XXV

Coyote and Chickadee

XXV

COYOTE AND CHICKADEE

WHILE roaming the hills one sun, looking for food, Coyote met Chickadee, who was carrying his elk-rib *shoo'-mesh* bow. Chickadee was very proud of his bow and the short stubby arrows that it used. Coyote thought he would like to have that bow, so he made fun of it.

"That bow is no good, *Zst-skaka'-na*," he said. "And such short, fat arrows. They cannot fly far—cannot kill anything. People will laugh at you for carrying such poor weapons. You had better throw them away."

"My bow and arrows may look poor and queer, but I like them," answered Chickadee. "And you think they cannot shoot far. I will show you. Go to the top of that ridge and walk slowly along it. Go there, and I will show you."

"I will go, silly *Zst-skaka'-na*," Coyote said. "That bow cannot put an arrow half way to the top of the ridge," and he started off. He was laughing.

Coyote felt gay. He trotted along, thinking about many foolish things, and by the time he reached the top of the ridge he had forgotten why he was there. He sang as he walked along the top of the ridge. He was enjoying the bright sunlight and the sweet smell of the air. All at once he heard a noise like that of a strange wind, and he stopped to listen.

"*Eh-ahe!*" he said. "That must be the spirits of other snows whispering to me." The words were but out of his mouth when one of Chickadee's arrows was in his ribs. It killed him.

Chickadee went after the arrow. He pulled it out, but he did not keep it. "*Caw!* I do not want that arrow. It smells bad," and he threw it away. He went on from there. He was going to a big council, a council of all the Animal People.

A few suns later Fox came upon the body of his twin brother. He knew that Coyote had been into mischief. He stepped over the body three times, and that brought Coyote to life.

"*Eh-ahe!* I have slept long, *Why-ay'-looh.*" Coyote yawned. "I was resting on this ridge."

"Yes, how long you have slept, *Sin-ka-lip'!* If I had not walked over your trail, you would have slept forever. You should know better than to contend with the little boy. His bow is powerful, and his arrows travel as the lightning. They reach the life, no matter the distance. My heart is sad with your mischief."

"Where did *Zst-skaka'-na* go?"

"He is on his way to the big council. The people are talking of making a trail to the Upper World Land," and with these words Fox left Coyote.

Coyote picked up the arrow that had killed him, and started after Chickadee. He followed fast on the trail, and in a few suns he caught up with Chickadee, who was quite surprised and not at all glad to see him.

"We shall gamble for the bow and the arrows," Coyote spoke. "We will throw arrows at a mark, not using the bow. The winner will take the weapons."

Chickadee had no wish to gamble, but Coyote coaxed and coaxed, and finally Chickadee said "All right." Chickadee thought he would win easily. But Coyote asked his *squas-tenk'* for help, and it moved Chickadee's eye from the mark when the boy threw an arrow. Chickadee could not hit the mark, and Coyote hit it every time, winning the stout bow and the powerful arrows. Then they gambled some more, and Chickadee lost his fine clothes of feathers, his weasel skins, and shell beads, even his hair ornaments—everything—and he was naked.

Coyote dressed in Chickadee's clothes and went his way. He took the bow and the arrows. He would go to the council camp of the Animal People and help them build a trail to the Upper

World Land, he said to himself. He was in fine humor. He threw his head from side to side to make the wampum rattle on his hair braids. He laughed at the picture of poor Chickadee, naked by the trail.

Pretty soon Coyote came to a small tepee. He heard children quarreling inside. He went in. No one was to be seen. By the fire were some red *kinnikinnick* berries. Coyote stepped outside the tepee and threw a stone along the ground. It made a noise like his walking on the trail. Then he peeked through the door-flap, and he saw a swarm of little children come out from beneath a bed of skin robes. The children began to quarrel again, over the best way to roast the red berries.

Coyote stepped back into the lodge. The children dove for their hiding place. All but one slipped under the skin robes. That one Coyote caught.

"Let me show you how to roast the berries," Coyote said. "Come out. I will not hurt you."

The children believed him. They came out. Coyote told them to bring all of the berries to him. He dug a hole in the coals of the fire, and, when the boys and girls started to hand the berries to him, he grabbed the children, too. Only one child got away and hid where Coyote could not find him. Coyote shoved the others into the coals to roast along with the berries. There he left them. As soon as Coyote had gone, the child that had escaped hurried to dig his brothers and sisters out of the coals, but they were dead.

Then Mother and Father *Se-qua'-quelt*— Prairie Chicken—came to the tepee. It was their home. They brought big packs of bugs and berries for their children. When they saw what had happened they sat down and cried. Chickadee was coming down the trail. He heard the crying. He went into the tepee to see if he could help. He felt sorry for the parents. He called to his mystery-power; he asked it to help him. Then he sprinkled ashes on the bodies of the children and stepped over them three times, and the little boys and girls came back to life. And they were as well and happy as if nothing had happened to them.

The parents wanted to pay Chickadee. He told them how Coyote had tricked him and taken his fine weapons and his good clothes. Right away Mother and Father Prairie Chicken guessed who had killed their children. They flew out of the tepee and followed Coyote's trail. Soon they caught up with him. They flew on by and to a high cliff above the river. There they hid and waited.

Singing, Coyote walked along. He felt good. But he was not to feel good very long, for, when he reached the edge of the cliff, Father Prairie Chicken flew at his face, and Mother Prairie Chicken darted between his legs. Blinded by the one and tripped by the other, Coyote lost his balance and pitched off the cliff. As he fell, the parents swooped after him and stripped off Chickadee's clothes and snatched away the medicine-bow and arrows, which they took to Chickadee, who started again for the council.

As he fell, spinning over and over, Coyote called to his *squas-tenk'*. *"Pess-pess qu-lupe!"* ("Come, come out!") he begged. "What shall I make myself into? A leaf?" Immediately he became a leaf, and the wind carried him high in the air and whirled him around and around until he was dizzy. He did not like that, so he said, "What now shall I make myself into—a pine needle?"

He became a pine needle and began to fall. Faster and faster he fell. He was almost to the river when he grew frightened and changed into cottonwood dust. Up again he was taken by the wind, wa-a-a-y up! The wind puffed him so high that he hardly could breathe. He did not like that. Once more he wished himself into a pine needle, and he fell, faster and faster, toward the river. Just above the water he wanted to slow up. He wanted to be a leaf again, but in his excitement he made a mistake. He wished himself into a *speks'-hene-men,* a pounding-rock (pestle), and he plunged—*ker-glump!*—to the bottom of the river.

There, on the bottom of the river, Coyote was helpless. He could not move, and he could not change into something else. His power was no good to him under water. After awhile he became hungry, and he was sitting like a rock, which he was, when along came *Enshap'-men-itqu*—Water-Bug.

"Take me to dry land," Coyote begged.

"I cannot drag you," Water-Bug answered. "You are much too heavy. I could not even budge you."

"Get all your relations," Coyote urged. "All of you working together can drag me out of this place. I will pay you well for your work."

So Water-Bug got all of his relatives to come and they pulled and tugged and pushed Coyote to dry land, and then he changed himself from a rock to his regular form. His heart was glad, and he gave all of the water-bugs hard coats of many colors, so that they could hide among the sharp river rocks. From that sun the water-bugs have had an easier life in their rock houses.

After he paid the water-bugs for their work, Coyote started once more for the council camp of the Animal People.

XXVI
The Arrow-Trail

THE ARROW-TRAIL

 **C**OYOTE was the last to arrive at the council camp of the Animal People. All the others were there. *Milka-noups*—Eagle, the strongest flier, had scouted to the Upper World Land and told of what he had seen there. A fine country, he said, full of wonders.

Eagle's talk made all the people eager to get up to that country high in the sky, where the best of the berries were thick on the bushes and hunting was easy—without the killing—and food of all kinds was plentiful.

The smartest persons from all over the world talked and schemed, trying to think of a way to reach the land in the sky. They talked and talked for many suns. Finally, someone suggested the shooting of arrows to make a trail through the sky. That thought was good, the council agreed. So the warriors and hunters tried to make an arrow trail. They shot arrow after arrow, but none of their bows were strong enough. All the arrows dropped back to earth. All tried and failed—all but little Chickadee.

Being small and modest, he waited until everyone else had tried. Then he strung his elk-rib *shoo'- mesh* bow. Everybody looked at him in surprise. They couldn't believe he really intended to shoot.

Chickadee said nothing, but he drew his bow as far as it would bend, and loosed a short stubby arrow, which flashed up out of sight and did not fall back. Then the little boy sent a second arrow after the first, and it did not come back. Then he shot a third and a fourth and a fifth and many, many more with his wonderful medicine-bow. Each arrow stuck into the one ahead of it, and the first arrow stuck into the Upper World Land. They made a long, straight ladder from the earth up to the mysterious country far above.

One by one, the people climbed up the ladder of arrows. The last to start was *Kee-lau-naw*— Grizzly Bear—who had been busy collecting food to take along. She was not satisfied with a little; she wanted to take a big pack of food. She had gathered wild rhubarb, skunk cabbage, and other plants she liked to eat. All that food made such a big pack that she hardly could swing it on her back. By the time Grizzly Bear began to climb, the others were in the Upper World Land. The arrow-trail creaked and groaned under the great weight of Grizzly Bear and the heavy pack of food. The higher she climbed, the more the ladder creaked. The strain on it became too much, and all at once there was a thunder-like crash, and the trail pulled loose from the Upper World Land. Down came the arrows, and down came Grizzly Bear. The fall did not kill her, but it gave her a bad shaking-up, and she was sore and lame for a long time.

Grizzly Bear's accident was not known to the others. They did not know their trail was destroyed. After their hard climb, they rested and congratulated themselves on reaching such a wonderful country. They were pleased to see so much food. It seemed to be everywhere.

Off in the distance they saw a big camp. They started toward it. They did not notice a scout that was watching them. The scout was a wise bird. He flew to the camp and told the people that enemies were coming, and the headmen of the village shouted: "The Lower Earth People have come to make war. Let us get ready for them."

So, when the Animal People got close to the camp they saw that the Upper World Land People were armed for war. That made them afraid. They did not want to fight in that strange country. They wanted peace. They sent Beaver, their wisest person, to talk and make peace. Beaver took a water-trail, where he was more at home. The trail led close to the camp, where Beaver heard a warrior say: "What shall we do with

Stun'-whu, the wisest of the earth people? He is coming along the water-trail. He is near."

That scared Beaver. He did not wait to hear more. He swam back as fast as he could. Then the people sent *Eut-la-who*—Raven—to talk peace. He flew low over the camp, but he did not alight, for he heard someone say: "What shall we do with *Eut-la-who*—Shiny Back? He is not liked even by his own people. Who will pierce him with an arrow?"

Well, Raven left in a hurry. One after another, the Animal People approached the camp to make peace, but the other people would have nothing to do with them. At last the Animal People gave up hope. The food that had appeared to be so plentiful was guarded by their enemies, and, as the suns passed, they became thin from hunger. They began to long for their old homes on earth. With sad hearts they turned back to the place where they thought the arrow-trail was fastened. *Eh-ahe!* It was gone! The only way down to earth was to jump, and it was a long, long jump. It was so far below that none could tell the color of the water or the color of the land.

Some jumped for what they thought was water, and some at what they guessed was land. *Qhu-quak*—Sucker—jumped at what looked like a patch of blue. It was water, but she missed it! She struck on the rocky bank of a river. And later, when high water came, Sucker's body was washed down the river. That restored her to life. But she was not the same as before. The fall to the rocky river bank broke all her bones— smashed them into splinters. That is why there are so many little bones in all suckers today. It is those splinter-like bones that make suckers hard to eat, that give them the name "choking-fish."

Sten-ten'-ywa, the Web-winged—Bat—was so excited when he jumped that he forgot to use his wings. He traveled to earth so fast that he was flattened right out when he hit the ground. He still can travel fast, but he is very ugly looking. He used to be handsome.

Coyote got down safely. First he turned himself into a pine needle, which fell fast. Then he became a leaf and floated gently to the ground. Then he resumed his own form.

After that time the Animal People were content to stay on earth, where they belonged. The breaking of their arrow-trail was the will of the Spirit Chief. He did not want the Animal People bothering the people of the Upper World Land again.

XXVII

Coyote Imitates Bear
and Kingfisher

XXVII

COYOTE IMITATES BEAR AND KINGFISHER

ONE TIME during the moons of snow, Coyote and Mole and their children were out of food. They were almost starved. Their nearest neighbors, *Skem-huist'*, the Claw-Grabber—Bear,[1] and Z-*reece'*—Kingfisher—had plenty to eat. Bear and Kingfisher always had plenty. Coyote knew this. He said to his wife: *"Pul'-laqu-whu,* I am going over the ridge and see your brother,[2] *Skem-huist'*. He may give me something for us to eat."

Coyote went to Bear's lodge. Bear and his wife had no children. Coyote noticed that they had nothing in their lodge but some bedding and a *klek'-chin* (cooking-basket). There were no signs of food, which made Coyote wonder. For awhile he sat in silence. Then he yawned. Bear knew what that meant. It was a hunger yawn.

---

[1] *Skem-huist,* the Claw-Grabber—the black or brown bear.

[2] Brother—Bear is not Mole's brother. Coyote speaks the word in its flattering sense. He employs it with like meaning in his later reference to Kingfisher.

Bear turned to his wife and said: "Put the rock in the fire and bring water in the basket. Your brother is hungry."

Bear's wife placed a rock in the fire and went after water. Coyote wondered where the food was to come from, and he yawned again. Bear's wife returned with the cooking-basket nearly full of water. Bear took his flint knife and cut a piece of buckskin from his wife's robe. He pressed the piece into a lump, and, when the rock in the fire was red-hot, he dropped the rock and the lump of buckskin into the cooking-basket. Then he rubbed ashes on his wife's robe, and the robe became whole again. It did not show where it had been cut.

As soon as the water in the basket boiled, Bear emptied a bag of pebbles into it. Coyote thought he wouldn't care for such food—buckskin and pebbles! But when the basket was placed before him, he tasted the food and quickly changed his mind; for the buckskin had become fine, tender meat, and the pebbles were juicy huckleberries!

Coyote ate all of the soup and the huckleberries and some of the meat, but he saved most of the meat for Mole and the children. "Let me carry this meat home in your cooking-basket," he said to Bear.

"All right," Bear answered. "You can send it back by one of your children." But Coyote insisted that Bear come for the basket, that he should come and visit him. Bear did not want to, but Coyote kept insisting until Bear said, "I will come for the basket."

The next sun Bear walked to Coyote's lodge. Seeing him coming down the ridge, Coyote had Mole hide all of their rose-hips that they had been eating for lack of better food. The rose-hips were famine food, eaten only in times of starving. Coyote also had Mole clean up the tepee so it would look like Bear's lodge, and beside the fire he had her leave only a cooking-basket, two sticks and a stone.

Looking in, Bear asked for his basket. He did not intend to go inside, but Coyote urged him to enter and sit down. Being polite, Bear did. Then Coyote told Mole to heat the stone in the fire and get a basket of water. Mole obeyed. When the stone was hot, Coyote took out his flint knife and cut a large piece of buckskin from Mole's robe—the only robe she owned. He pressed the piece into a lump, as he had seen Bear do, and he told Mole to put it and the hot stone in the cooking-basket. Using the two sticks as tongs, Mole lifted the stone from the fire and dropped it in the water along with the lump of buckskin. As Bear had done to his wife's robe, Coyote rubbed ashes on Mole's spoiled robe, but it did not become whole again. It remained as he had cut it. Mole felt bad. Then Coyote poured pebbles from a bag into the boiling water. Soon all sat up to eat, but only tough buckskin and hard pebbles were taken from the basket. Coyote said nothing. He was ashamed. After awhile Bear spoke. *"Sin-ka-lip',"* he said, "this is my way, not yours. You cannot do what I can, and I do not try to imitate people as you do."

Then Bear rubbed ashes on Mole's robe and it was as good as ever. Bear picked up his own cooking-basket and went home. Pretty soon Coyote looked into his cooking-basket. What he saw made him grunt with surprise. Instead of buckskin and pebbles, there was plenty of good meat and huckleberries. He laughed.

For many suns Coyote and Mole and their children lived on the meat and the berries that Bear had made for them with his magic power. When all of that food was eaten and they were hungry once more, Coyote said:

"Pul'-laqu-whu, I am going to see your brother, *Z-reece'.* Maybe he will give us something to eat," and he went to Kingfisher's tepee. Invited in, he entered and sat down. He saw nothing to eat in there. He yawned. Kingfisher knew what that meant, and he spoke to the older of his two children. "My son," he said, "go and bring me three willows."

Boy Kingfisher went out. He returned soon

with three willow sticks, which Kingfisher took
and heated over the fire. When they were hot,
he twisted them to make them strong and tied
them to his belt. Then he flew to the top of the
lodge and from there to the river, where he
dove through a hole in the ice. He came up with
the willow sticks strung with fish. These were
for his neighbor, Coyote. Kingfisher's wife
cooked the fish. Coyote ate his fill, but some
were left for him to take to Mole and the children. "May I carry these fish home in your
cooking-basket?" he asked.

"Yes, take the basket," said Kingfisher. "Send
it back by one of your children."

"No, I want you to visit me," Coyote replied.
"You come over tomorrow and get the basket."

Kingfisher had no wish to visit Coyote, but
Coyote coaxed him and at last he agreed, and the
next sun he walked to Coyote's lodge.

"My son," said Coyote to the eldest of his sons,
as Kingfisher sat down, "go and bring me three
willows."

"What do you want them for?" Boy Coyote
asked. "How will you use them?"

"You must know why I want three willows,"
Coyote scolded. "You always have brought
them to me."

Boy Coyote said nothing more. He went out
and got three willow sticks, and his father heated

them over the fire and twisted them, as he had seen Kingfisher do. He tied the sticks to his belt and tried to fly to the top of the lodge; he had a hard time climbing there without breaking down the whole tepee. From the lodge-top he jumped for a hole in the river ice. He missed the hole and smashed on the ice and was killed.

Kingfisher had been watching from the doorway and smiling to himself. He walked over to where Coyote lay. Taking the willow sticks from Coyote's belt, he tied them to his own belt and dove through the hole in the ice. When he came up he had the willow sticks heavy with fish. These he placed beside Coyote and stepped over him three times. That brought Coyote back to life.

Then Kingfisher said: "This is my way, not yours, *Sin-ka-lip'*. I do not try to imitate others, as you do."

Kingfisher took his basket and went home, and Coyote went back to his tepee. He carried the fish that Kingfisher had caught. He gave them to Mole to cook.

"See! We have plenty to eat now," Coyote laughed. "We have plenty for my imitating Bear and Kingfisher. That is why I imitated them!"

NOTES ON THE STORIES

Mourning Dove called her collection *Okanogan Sweat House,* in homage to the leader of the Animal Spirit People living before Coyote started his transformations. As a living oral literature, these stories have no set form. Their telling depends on narrative skill, audience, and circumstances. Among elders, they are aesthetic treasures in measured verse, yet when told to children, they are abbreviated. The merit of a story rests on the completeness and sensitive patterning of its text, texture, and context. At its fullest, a story is also localized in place and time, ending with an edict about how conditions got to be as they are now.

Other examples of Salishan Plateau stories, legends, tales, and sagas have been published,[1] but these lack details of texture, context, and performance. Mourning Dove's story drafts have also been published,[2] devoid of commentary or insight. These drafts, along with letters, reside in the McWhorter Collection.[3]

Recent scholarship has emphasized the importance of language, performance, and creativity for understanding oral literature. Linguists interested in the dramatic patterning of the text have contributed much, along with accurate representations for the names of mythic characters.[4]

I. Spirit Chief Names the Animal People

A more esoteric version of Naming Day is given in the Introduction, with fuller explanations of the special nature of Coyote's power. This naming properly leads off this collection since it remains the chartering saga for many of the Interior Salishan tribes to this day. Belief in the Chief Above, while since influenced by Christianity, was indeed aboriginal in the

Plateau and other regions of the Americas.[5] The origin of Sweatlodge from the wife of the Spirit Chief is a unique feature of this account and has not been satisfactorily explained. Mourning Dove may have intended a feminist stance, or she may have been influenced by Flathead belief in Sweatlodge as Grandmother.

Creation was not an issue among the Salishans. As with many other oral traditions, they simply accepted that the world had always existed, although variously modified by Coyote and others. Today, due to Biblical influence, the creation of the world has been described. James Teit collected origin stories from the Okanagans, explaining the creation of Earth Woman, Sky, and Underworld through the efforts of Chief Above. Among these three planes, "All are connected by a pole or tree which passes through the middle of each."[6] In another recent version, the connecting axis is an apple tree, a wry comment on the role of Colvilles in the current Washington State apple industry.

Similarly, human arrival is simply accepted. Among the Methows, however, humans were created by Coyote from slices cut from a monster Beaver who rampaged along the Columbia River.

II. Fox and Coyote and Whale

In a similar story, the monster is a giant Otter who lived in the Columbia near Orondo, Washington. Other monsters represented sturgeon, which are indeed enormous in the Columbia. Throughout the Northwest, Mouse is known as a polyglot, a symbolic consequence of the ability of mice to live everywhere, from homes to fields.

III. Coyote Fights Some Monsters

This is a typical series of adventures, told separately or in mixed order, depending on constraints of time and place. Each episode ends with the commandment issued by Coyote establishing the conditions as they are now known to humans. The horse was, however, an historic import to the Plateau, greatly facilitating bison hunting on the Plains.

IV. Chipmunk and Owl

This remains a well-known story, and a likely inspiration for the relations between the grandmother and heroine in Mourning Dove's novel, whose title is taken from the Okanogan word for Chipmunk. Children are still urged to behave by threats of a visit from Sneena.[7] A character type known as Basket Ogress, Sneena was the prototype for the present species of Great Horned Owl. Missing from this version is the usual explanation that Sneena's lower jaw was ripped off and thrown into the water, where it turned into the species of waterfowl known as coots, which swim together in the distinctive parabolic pattern of a jawbone.

V. Coyote and the Buffalo

The concern with modesty by Mourning Dove and her editors is exemplified by this story. According to all other accounts, Coyote took his revenge by urinating in addition to spitting, kicking, and insulting the bison skull. Missing from this version is the explanation that Coyote stuck his cane into the last tree to hold it steady and thus supplied heartwood to future trees. It was just this heartwood that Coyote later used to make stronger, sharper horns for the old bull.

VI. Why Flint-Rock Cannot Fight Back

In this version, hints remain of the nature of Coyote's medicine powers. When they refuse to help him, he threatens them with a downpour. The native audience would realize what disastrous consequences rain would have for feces and so understand their reconsideration and aid. The color of the dress worn by Mole to attract Flint was described by Charles Quintasket, Mourning Dove's half-brother, as the color of a boiled crayfish shell.

VII. How Turtle Got His Tail

This story represents a native retelling of the Aesop fable about the Hare and the tortoise. Since meeting whites, Colvilles and others have been hearing European stories, making them their own[8] and using them to explain features of their own experience.

VIII. Why Skunk's Tail Is Black and White

In oral literature, Skunk is an extremely dangerous, but also hilarious, character. In this version he is atypically portrayed because, as Mourning Dove often said, if she wrote Skunk stories as they traditionally were told, the authorities would "put her in jail." To appreciate her remark, such a Skunk story has been added after these notes.

IX. Rattlesnake and Salmon

While Mourning Dove placed this story at Kettle Falls and among the Kalispel, the Methows locate it further down the Columbia River. They say that the chief at Pateros arranged a contest whose winner would marry his daughter. Salmon won over five (or, more recently, three) Wolf brothers, who sought revenge. Rattlesnake took their side and killed Salmon with an arrow, while the Wolf brothers made off with the wife. Salmon floated downriver, revived in the ocean (without the aid of Mouse), and returned to revenge himself on the Wolves and Snake. Though curiously ignored in this variant, Salmon's widow was the first Mourning Dove. Every Spring, until prevented by the dams, mourning doves calling along the banks of the river signaled to the Salishans that the salmon had returned. A token arrowpoint remains in the head of each salmon, a proof of the shot from a craggy island in the Columbia, now partially submerged behind Rocky Reach Dam, marking the petrified home of Rattlesnake.

X. Coyote Meets Wind and Some Others

Although the Hemp sisters appear here as minor characters, plants are important in the oral tradition.[9] At Naming Day, Bitterroot was the first plant to speak, offering to be the first food of spring. Modesty prevented Mourning Dove from explaining that Coyote created the obscuring fog by ejaculating.

XI. Why Gartersnake Wears a Green Blanket

A European account of St. George and the Dragon was probably the inspiration for this version, but it builds upon a widespread Native American belief in the eternal antagonism between Sky and Water, Thunderbird and Seamonster.

XII. Coyote Quarrels with Mole

This is a segment of a series showing Coyote at his worst. He was too lazy and slow to feed his family, and Mole, for once, objected before fleeing for her life. He was left with five sons to care for, and they all were soon starving. While he killed and ate the older ones, he spared the youngest child, Topqn.[10]

XIII. How Coyote Happened to Make Black Moss Food

Coyote and his son continued on, tried to take beaver or swan, but were bested. The Animal People knew that Coyote had wronged his family, so they were not sympathetic to his hunger. In the process, the son's ears were stretched, so all coyotes now have long ears. The moss that was created from his hair is still a favorite food of Colvilles, who have devised ways of baking it in stove ovens instead of the traditional pit ovens (described in footnote 3, pp. 124–25).

XIV. Why Spider Has Such Long Legs

Spider was punished for his vanity, although he contributed to the public welfare. Beaver's daughter thrived because she was encased in deerskin that acted as a fresh air chamber.

XV. Why Badger Is So Humble

In Salishan folklore, Badger is consummately slow and clumsy. His brief moment of glory ends in humiliation. In other regions, the character refusing marriage is a haughty girl, who usually falls for a handsome man who was a Snake. In this version, the pretty woman was Coyote, a further example of his versatility.

XVI. Coyote Juggles His Eyes

This story is well known throughout the Plateau. The Yakima Coyote (Speelyi) used a flower (still known as Coyote's eyes) as a substitute until he could retrieve his own sight. Among the Colvilles, the bird whose eyes were stolen and replaced with huckleberries is the rufus-sided Towee, which has tiny red eyes. Traditionally, when the Bird sisters attempted to carry the disguised Coyote on their backs, they kept throwing him down not because he made himself an awkward burden but because he was attempting to fondle and penetrate them.

XVII. Why Marten's Face Is Wrinkled

Marten comes off as totally inept. He did not know how to eat venison and grease, he disobeyed his older brother, and he violated the laws of hospitality by refusing the girl's offered food.

XVIII. Crawfish and Grizzly Bear

Because people had danced and prayed, Crayfish, otherwise insignificant, was empowered to best Grizzly Bear. Because

236

bears led summer and winter lives, they had two sets of teeth, which, along with hide and claws, they wore over their human form. It is interesting that Grizzly stayed in the highest mountains because of a promise, not an edict.

XIX. Coyote and Wood-tick

The role of Wood-tick as deer warden emphasizes the need for a cautious respect of nature, where even the most minuscule can have great power. In another modern story, Wood-tick and Ant were riding a wagon that turned over, giving Wood-tick a flat, shiny head. Grieving, Ant kept tightening her belt so that all ants now have tiny waists.

XX. Why Mosquitos Bite People

Unlike other stories, this one uses the traditional number, five. In other versions, mosquitos were created from the ashes of a cremated blood-sucking monster.

XXI. The Gods of Sun and Moon

This story picks up the lives of Mole and Coyote after they separated, correctly noting that Mole "made love" to the rock and root, begetting Warm Red Rock and White Root as replacements for the sons whom Coyote had eaten. After Coyote and Mole were reconciled, they heard about the council to select the Sun and Moon. According to the usual version, the brothers went downriver to the meeting. Along the way, they had to contend with the doglike Monster who lived at Ribbon Cliff on the west side of the Columbia. Fatally wounded, the monster ran around spewing blood, leaving the dark bands which give that rock its English name.

At the council, all of the other contenders had been rejected. For example, Crane was so long that his beak was beginning to set before his toes had left the ground. Coyote called out all that he saw from the sky, mostly illicit relations. As the brothers prepared to try, Frog brought on the rain and lured them into her house. There, as described, White Root refused her offer of marriage and the insulted Frog jumped onto his face and remained there. The final outcome was that Red Rock became the Sun and White Root became the Moon, even now marked by the dark patch of Frog Woman.

Mourning Dove made reference to this story in her novel: "if you place a frog on its back . . . she will look up at the sun and flirt with him . . . He hates her so badly," he will cause it to rain.[11]

XXII. Porcupine Learns the Sun-Dance

Despite its familiar name, the Plateau tribes did not have the Sun Dance traditionally, although tribes along the border with the Plains adopted it historically along with the horse and other features made stereotypical of all Indians by Hollywood films.

XXIII. En-am-tues—The Wishing Stone

Though blasted apart, the fragments of the Hee-hee stone are well known and even appear on a popular postcard. Needless to say, Colvilles regard her as a local girl rather than one of Ka-lispel origin. Similar stories are told of other mountains in the region. Along the coast, Mounts Rainier, Adams, and Baker were once a husband and two wives who separated after a dispute.

XXIV. Chickadee Makes a Shoo-Mesh Bow

Colvilles are very fond of tiny Chickadee and his powerful elk-rib bow, using him as a reminder that great things can come in tiny packages.

XXV. Coyote and Chickadee

Though unexplained, the ending of this story is premised on the commandment of Story II that the Land People and the

Water People have become forever separated. Thus, Coyote had to convince the Waterbugs to roll him out of the river; otherwise he could not summon his own help. His powers would have dissolved in the water.

XXVI. The Arrow Trail

Better known as the Arrow Chain, this is a widespread story that is often used to bring down the curtain on the Mythic Age. Supposedly, people went to the Sky World to get fire. In modern tellings, Mrs. Grizzly Bear broke the chain because she tried to take up everything she owned: her food, pots, pans, and microwave oven. Those who did make it up, had to jump down, as described. Suckers (a variety of fish) are indeed bony, and Bats wrinkled. Within Washington State, this episode is also used to explain why there are only harmless snakes west of the Cascade Mountains, while rattlesnakes occur east of them. Elders say that all snakes used to be everywhere, but, jumping from the sky, rattlers landed in the sagebrush country and gartersnakes among the evergreens.

XXVII. Coyote Imitates Bear and Kingfisher

The theme of this story is better known as Bungling Host. By ending with it, Mourning Dove reminds us that Coyote survived the visit to the sky and many other adventures. He lives on, having learned how important it is to "be yourself," an affirmation of the value of different lifeways.

NOTES

1. Charles Hill-Tout, *The Natives of British North America I: The Far West, the Home of the Salish and Dene* (London: Archibald Constable and Co., 1907); Hill-Tout, "Report on the Ethnology of the Okanakan of British Columbia, an Interior Division of the Salish Stock," *Journal of the Royal Anthropological Institute*, 41 (1911): 130–61; Marian K. Gould on Okanagon and

Sanpoil tales in Franz Boas, *Folk-Tales of Salishan and Sahaptin Tribes,* Memoirs of the American Folklore Society, Vol. 11 (1917), pp. 98–118; James A. Teit on Okanagon tales in Boas, pp. 65–97; Verne Ray, "Sanpoil Folk Tales," *Journal of American Folklore,* 46 (1933): 129–87; *Coyote and the Colville,* ed. Eileen Yanan (Omak, Wash.: St. Mary's Mission, 1971); Harry Robinson, *Write It on Your Heart. The Epic World of an Okanagan Storyteller.* Compiled and edited by Wendy Wickwire (Vancouver, British Columbia: Talon Books, 1989).

2. *Tales of the Okanogans,* ed. Donald M. Hines (Fairfield, Wash.: Ye Galleon Press, 1976).

3. Nelson Ault, The Papers of Lucullus Virgil McWhorter, Pullman: Friends of the Washington State University Library, 1959.

4. Anthony Mattina, *Colville-Okanagan Dictionary,* University of Montana Occasional Papers in Linguistice no. 5.

5. Jay Miller, "High-Minded High Gods in North America," *Anthropos* 75 (1980): 916–19.

6. Boas, p. 84.

7. Compare *Tales of the Okanogans,* p. 103.

8. Compare Mattina, *The Golden Woman: The Colville Narrative of Peter J. Seymour* (Tucson: University of Arizona Press, 1985).

9. Nancy Turner, Randy Bouchard, and Dorothy Kennedy, *Ethnobotany of the Okanagan-Colville Indians of British Columbia and Washington,* Occasional Paper 21, 1980, British Columbia Provincial Museum, Victoria.

10. Compare *Tales of the Okanogans,* p. 86.

11. Mourning Dove, *Cogewea, The Half Blood. A Depiction of the Great Montana Cattle Range* (1927; reprint, Lincoln: University of Nebraska Press, 1981), p. 159.

APPENDIX: Additional Stories

Absent from the book and the published drafts are three other stories recalled by Charles Quintasket, Christine's half-brother, who read through her collection in 1930 when he was twenty-one years old and was staying with Christine and Fred. Her draft of the Skunk story[1] lacks the detail and placement of that presented here. Now that native literature has been accepted in its own right, Skunk stories have been published without anyone "going to jail." An uncensored Skunk story, profusely illustrated, appears in Hilbert.[2]

A. Why Dogs Sniff

Dog People were catching and drying salmon. One morning, they got up to find that all of their supply was gone. Everyone got suspicious of everyone else and began to sniff each other's butts to learn who had eaten salmon. They never found out who the thief was, but they are still looking.

B. Coyote and the Swans

Coyote was going around. He heard that the Swan brothers had a sister who was a virgin, so he decided to introduce her to the mysteries of life. He wished for a disguise: a beautiful buckskin outfit, a white weaselskin headband, and a handsome appearance. He became a fine example of Lakes manhood and went to visit the Swans.

The five brothers were away, but the sister made him welcome, offering him food. As she passed it to him, he pushed it back, acting haughty. When the brothers returned, they were impressed by his pride. All of them, that is, except the youngest brother, who was sure he smelled "old stink Coyote." The others, convinced that the Lakes man was a prize catch, urged their sister to accept him. And so Coyote married the virgin.

The Swan brothers always hunted in the highest mountains around the Arrow Lakes because those animals had the choicest meat. For his own reasons, the new brother-in-law wanted to go along. The youngest brother, of course, objected, but the oldest brother agreed. The brothers flew off, the eldest carrying Coyote, and left him on the shore of the lake. Then they flew high into the mountains and were soon out of sight.

Coyote changed back into himself and began to pound on the ground. Soon, moles began to come out and Coyote caught them, singed them in the fire, and shoved them down his throat. He ate his fill of moles, his favorite food, even though they were relatives of his ever-faithful wife.

The Swan brothers would announce their return by honking from a long way away, making a great spiral on the way down to the beach. By the time they landed, Coyote had turned back into a Lakes dandy, the fire was out, and the moles were gone. The older brothers carried Coyote home because the youngest one would have nothing to do with "stink Coyote."

After they had been home for a time, they would go back to hunt, leaving their brother-in-law at the beach. This went on for months, with the youngest brother growing more and more suspicious. Finally, he decided to unmask Coyote on the next trip.

Again, they went hunting and took their brother-in-law along, leaving him on the shore. When they had vanished, he turned back into Coyote and ate lots of moles. By now, the brothers were tired of always packing him along and decided to test their younger brother's warnings. Gliding silently downward, they looked far into the distance to see Coyote in his true form, eating moles. Disgusted, now they believed the youngest Swan.

Flying back to the mountain tops, they made a plan and returned honking. Coyote heard them so, when they landed, he was back in the form of a gay blade, although the brothers knew now that he was really Coyote. They picked him up, without letting on that they knew who he was, flew to the middle of the lake, and dropped him cold.

Coyote thought quickly and decided to change himself into a leaf. Saying the word, however, he pronunciated it, turned into a rock instead, and sank to the bottom of Upper Arrow Lake. When fish and bugs came to inspect the new arrival, Coyote was full of promises, asking them to help him. Finally, the fish and bugs pushed him to shore.

Once he was on dry land, he changed himself back into Coyote and trotted toward the home of the Swans. When he got to the hill above their house, he shouted, "Coyote left a baby in the virgin." The Swans were ashamed because all of their safeguarding of family honor had come to naught. And then Coyote went on.

C. Skunk

An old woman had two granddaughters, Chipmunk and Rock Squirrel. They all lived together. The girls had a boyfriend. He was Fisher. One day they heard the ominous sound of Skunk coming: phuw. phuw. phuw. phuw. phuw. He kept breaking wind. They could hear him coming. The old woman hid the girls in the place they used for emergencies like this.

He came there and looked around. He said, "Where are the girls?" The woman concocted some story about why they weren't there, maybe they were off berry picking. He did not believe her. Skunk was the most dangerous man in the Animal Kingdom. Nobody messed with him. When he started looking around for the girls, the woman stayed away.

Skunk found the girls. He found them by golly. He said, "Come with me girls," and they took off. They went on like that. Nightfall overtook them and they found shelter in a cave. He slept between the girls.

Meanwhile Fisher came over to see his girlfriends. The grandmother tearfully told him what had happened. The great

Skunk had taken the girls with him. Fisher went after them. He followed the scent and caught up with them at the cave. Skunk was sound asleep. Snoring and blasting.

Fisher whispered "tsmps" to get the girls' attention. They were pretty desperate, hoping that he would follow after them. He motioned for them to come out. Easy and quiet, they got out. One at a time. They got loose and came out to him. Of course, Fisher was a medicine man, too. He had powers of his own. He made the cave close in on Skunk. He and the girls took off. If he had left well enough alone, there would not have been any further story. But Fisher wanted to crush that guy.

All at once, the ceiling was like to close in on Skunk. He thought the girls were snuggling up to him. He said in Skunkese, through his nose, "Get over. Move over. You must love me too well." Finally, just when he was going to be crushed to a pulp, he smartened out, "Hell, this cave is going to crush me." He tried to zip out, but it was too late. He got as far as the entrance, but it was only a small hole. He said, "Gee, How am I going to get out?" He decided that the only way was to take himself apart.

He took off his legs, his head, his shoulders, his hips, and, last of all, his rear end. He was especially careful with his ahso. That was his atomic bomb. He held on to that. It was his most precious part. It made him what he was and made everyone else fearful. He could not lose it. Then he would be nobody. Most carefully, he started to stick it through the hole, but then he heard Ravens, so he would pull it back. He could not let the Ravens have it.

The cave was still closing up, but more slowly. Skunk had to decide what he would do. The rest of him was already outside and needed to be protected from the Ravens. By gosh, he was getting pretty desperate. He had to take a chance. He thought that if he would leap out and put himself together, he could sit down and protect his valuable end. He called out threateningly, "I'll sit on that atomic bomb so Raven can't get it."

That was his plan. He had to do it. He got ready, threw out the ahso, and got himself together.

But he was not quick enough. A Raven had swooped down and taken his rear end. The Ravens flew back to the village and everyone began to play with Skunk's asset.

Skunk did not feel right and felt himself all over. When he got to the back, he realized that something was missing. He saw the Ravens fly off with it. He followed them. Finally, after a long search, he found a bunch of kids using his ahso as a hoop. They were rolling it in the dark and watching it flash. Phuw. Phuw. Phuw. Phuw. Phuw. That's the flash. It was something to watch.

Skunk had to figure a way of getting his asset back. "Now, how am I going to do it?" He thought out a scheme. He waited until the kids rolled the hoop back. Then he ran alongside it and when it fell over, he sat on it. As soon as he sat down, all systems were go. He was recharged. He used his dog-gone power. He turned the dangerous end of himself onto the crowd. He just mowed them down. Yeah, they all fell down.

Now he was ready to start tracking Fisher and the girls. He finally caught up with them just this side of where the town of Colville, Washington is now. They call that place, "blasted in front of the face." There is a little spring there, right at the bottom of the cliff. Skunk was looking down when he saw them. He started blasting at them. Nothing happened. He tried again and again. Finally, he looked up and saw them up on the cliff. Heck, he was shooting at their reflections. Now he tried shooting at them, but he fell short. He was almost out of ammunition. He started chewing grass and recouped. He was ready, acting like a darned machine gun. All of them missed, except for a tiny spray that just touched Fisher's toe. Down he came. Tumbling down and dead.

Skunk got those girls by saying, "You guys are next if you don't come down." They did not like him, but they did not want to die either. So, down they came. They must have married on the spot. Skunk ended up in Wonderland.

It is funny, you know. There are still three stony figures on that cliff, above that spring, across the road from where the Drive-In is now. When you are doing east toward Colville, you can not see those stone columns, but coming west along the road, they are plain as day. You can see their outline against the cliff. Of course, the big one is Fisher. Chipmunk and Rock Squirrel are the little ones. They are still there to this day, proving this story.

NOTES

1. *Tales of the Okanogans,* ed. Donald M. Hines (Fairfield, Wash.: Ye Galleon Press, 1976).

2. Vi Taqsheblu Hilbert, *Haboo. Native American Stories from Puget Sound* (Seattle: University of Wasington Press, 1985), pp. 158–63.